The Old Ways
Volume 1

Curated by Holley Cornetto
Edited by S.O. Green

EERIE RIVER PUBLISHING

The Old Ways: Volume 1

Eerie River Publishing
www.EerieRiverPublishing.com
Hamilton, Ontario Canada
This book is a work of fiction. Names, characters, places, events,
organizations and incidents are either part of the author's imagination
or are used fictitiously. Any resemblance to actual persons, living or
dead, or actual events is purely coincidental.

ISBN: 978-1-990245-89-3

Edited by S.O. Green
Curated by Holley Cornetto
Cover Design Michelle River

ORIGINAL STORIES BY

Bradley Don Richter
Stephanie Ellis
Patrick Barb
Teagan Olivia Sturmer
TJ Price
Bitter Karella
April Yates
E.S. Corble
Julie Sevens
Keily Blair
Ryan Marie Ketterer
Wynne F. Winters
S.O. Green
Jonathan Louis Duckworth

STORIES

TRIGGER WARNINGS MAY INCLUDE DEATH, ABUSE, MURDER, OCCULTISM, RITUALISTIC TORTURE, DEATH OF A CHILD AND ANIMALS AND MENTION OF SEXUAL ASSAULT.

A FROLIC IN THE DIGITAL WOOD:

THE ROMANTICISM OF FOLK HORROR

When Romanticism swept the western world at the turn of the nineteenth century, the art filled a void, provided voices, and patched souls. Against the backdrop of an Industrial Revolution—a time when rural people were uprooted, with urban sprawls replacing green fields—Romanticism provided a reaction to what was lost. If your window gave narrow views of brick and soot, a Wordsworth poem, by contrast, treated your mind's eye to idyllic vistas and serene lakes—a mental frolic in the face of drudgery, as it were, or a dance in the face of loss.

Romanticism is an art for times of great change.

Of course, this categorization risks the label of escapism, a term equated with intellectual insolvency. Escapism, however, isn't always about fleeing into the imaginary countryside. Escapism also allows us to confront deeper anxieties about change. Even when escapism colludes with imagination rather than reason, it provides a window for understanding ourselves.

Folk Horror, too, is an art for times of great change.

From its emphasis on nature to the exploration of folkways, prejudices, and paganism, Folk Horror shares a great deal with Romanticism. Both movements provide the dual release of escapism and confrontation. Folk Horror, too, has blossomed against similarly trying backdrops of change.

The first Folk Horror boom began in the 1960s when the western world reeled, confronting the folly of war and the absence of civil rights. Our current Folk Horror revival occurs in a time where we battle great inequalities, while also experiencing a Digital (rather than Industrial) Revolution. In this latest uprooting, the unreal is replacing the real, and the unpalpable is supplanting the tactile. The vast internet, a digital forest, awaits us each day. This is an anemic existence for many, so the Janus-faced desire to retreat and confront is reborn, just as the desire emerged circa 1800.

Like the Romanticism of old, the art of Folk Horror can provide a voice and patch a soul, filling the void. Here moldering bones refuse to stay buried, things taken are reclaimed, tensions erupt between old and new, and rural Arcadias succumb to inspection. Through Folk Horror, we escape and confront a digital Hellscape rather than an industrial one, but the desired outcome is the same.

In The Old Ways, Holley Cornetto and S.O. Green have gathered tales that equal a frolic in this digital wood we travel, granting us escape while also delivering horrors that articulate our anxieties and confront the issues of life in the twenty-first century.

It's a superb collection. I hope you enjoy the dance.

Coy Hall
Author of Grimoire of the Four Impostors
West Virginia, USA
January 2023

SCARECROW

By Bradley Don Richter

In San Cuervo, California, a boy is not a man until he's smoked Scarecrow.

Every year, on Halloween night, Sam Marshall puts up the scarecrow in his fallow field. Only he doesn't stuff it with straw.

He stuffs it with what folks in San Cuervo call Scarecrow, an herb he grows on his land and dries in his barn, an herb that smells like skunk spray.

They say it opens your eyes. Eyes you didn't know you had. And reveals to you the Crow.

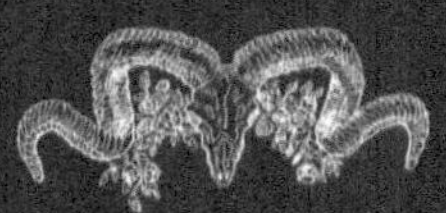

Joe saw it once. Not the Crow—the Scarecrow growing. He knew it was a risk, but he had to see it before his eighteenth Halloween, to know if the town elders spoke true.

Joe rode his bike up to the top of Acorn Ridge, a hill overlooking Sam Marshall's farm, on the afternoon of the Fourth of July, his eighteenth birthday. He pumped the pedals, tasting copper in the back of his throat, wishing his mom had bought him the ten-speed he'd wanted.

July's kiln was sweltering. He peeled off his t-shirt and felt the beads of his effort evaporate in the afternoon breeze as he stared down at San Cuervo. He could see everything from up here, but Covered Bridge Park was most prominent. He watched a bunch of kids swing and slide and hide and seek. How many years until their eighteenth birthdays?

Lucky brats, Joe thought. *They'll be even luckier if they die before their eighteenth Halloween.*

He grabbed his binoculars and aimed them at Old Man Marshall's farm. He'd heard that the Scarecrow needed dappled sunlight to thrive, so he scanned Marshall's farm until he saw a latticework structure, vined with thorny briar. He crept along the ridge, staring at the magnified circles hovering before his eyes, until he saw a lattice gate hanging open. Marshall emerged, a hoe over his right shoulder and a bag of fertilizer cradled in his left arm.

He seemed to stare right at Joe.

Joe lowered the binoculars. His heart galloped in his chest. When he found the courage to bring them back up to his eyes, Sam Marshall was gone.

He scanned until he spotted Marshall again. The old man now emerged from a shed with a watering can in one hand and a pair of garden shears in the other. Joe watched as the hunched geezer crept back into the latticework structure, leaving the gate open behind him.

Joe had never seen Marshall up close. Few had, except for some select elders, of which Marshall was the oldest. He had a crazed white beard and wore hand-sewn slacks and nothing else. Even his feet were bare, black and calloused, the toenails curled up into calcified claws. His arms were knotty with muscles from a lifetime of farming. All the spit dried up in Joe's mouth as he took in Old Man Marshall's most striking feature: his wholeness.

Every man over the age of eighteen in San Cuervo was... missing something.

Every man, that is, except for Sam Marshall.

Joe could only look at the old man—the *whole* man—for a second before turning away.

When he turned back, he saw the Scarecrow growing. There were maybe fifty plants. The stalks were about as thick as Joe's thumb and the most vibrant green he'd ever seen. Massive, six-fingered leaves fanned out, the plant's natural latticework. Then he saw the buds—long, tight, purple flowers with tiny yellow hairs that looked like they'd been dusted with diamonds. He'd seen a lot of flowers in his life, but he'd never seen anything as unusual as Scarecrow, nor as beautiful. The sour-sweet smell of it rode a hot summer wind up the hill, right up his nostrils.

He watched Old Man Marshall water the plants and trim the leaves for a few minutes, then he crammed the binoculars into his backpack and rode home.

Joe wasn't sure what madness had driven him to risk catching a glimpse of the Scarecrow in bloom. He wouldn't dare whisper a word of it to anyone.

But after he saw it, he felt calmer.

And he was a little less frightened of Halloween night.

Joe's mother had a party for him that night. She'd done it seventeen years running, so why miss the eighteenth—and possibly the last, Joe and everyone else tried not to think as they sipped flat, cheap beer from a tepid keg. Joe's father snuck him a red Solo cup full of it late in the evening. He chugged it, even though it tasted like lukewarm piss.

Joe didn't give a crap about the party, the blackened hot dogs, the pity beers. He was sick of hearing his mother's vapid friends blather on about how proud they were of Joe, as if he and the other eighteeners had done anything special aside from being born male in San Cuervo and living to see their eighteenth birthdays. And if he never had to shake another crushing hand or be pulled into the stale cologne of another man-hug from one of his father's friends, he figured he could die happy—a thought that made him instantly unhappy.

The harsh fact was: he could die on Halloween.

He could die in seventeen weeks.

One hundred nineteen days.

Two thousand eight hundred fifty-six hours.

He'd done the math. Too many times. Burned out the batteries in his calculator.

He liked the number of minutes because it was beyond anything he could really picture. The seconds were even better. It seemed like there were so many of them.

But the seconds and the minutes were already bleeding into hours. Soon, the hemorrhaging hours would become days, weeks, months...

And that's where it ended. That's where it *could* end.

The numbers plagued him as he suffered through the lame party. The numbers, and thoughts of Mary, his new girlfriend. She told him she had a surprise waiting for him after the party, and the way she said it, he knew exactly what she meant. At least, he hoped he did.

The party ended, and his parents' annoying friends went home. He made some small talk with his mother and father until the white wines and whiskeys they'd respectively been knocking back finally knocked *them* back. They passed out on the couch in front of the muted TV, playing a marathon of old war movies. How patriotic.

He slipped out of the house and met Mary at her place. Her parents were out of town. She answered the door wearing a black negligee.

"Where's my present?" he asked.

She took his hands and placed them on her hips. "Why don't you unwrap it?"

He did—and he took his sweet time doing it.

A little less than four months later, on the night before Halloween, Joe sat in his room talking on the phone to Mary.

More accurately, he was playing Call of Duty on Xbox. Mary was talking to him.

Screeching, really.

"Why aren't we together tonight? Halloween is tomorrow!"

Joe grunted, distracted by the game.

"Are you even listening to me, Joseph?"

He hit pause. Sighed. "Of course I'm listening to you."

"Good. Then maybe you'll hear this." But she didn't say anything more.

A minute or two went by. Joe wasn't sure how long. He had un-paused the game as soon as she'd started talking and had gone back into battle.

"You still there?" he asked, but he didn't really care one way or the other.

He sensed that she wanted to talk about something serious, and there was nothing more serious than becoming a man in San Cuervo. But it was pointless to spend time thinking about it. The Crow was going to take what the Crow was going to take. If that was going to be his fate, so be it. He was better off not thinking about it.

Because thinking about it meant thinking about running.

His bag was already packed. He could take his father's truck. Or hitchhike.

But he couldn't run. Could he? In theory, he could. But *would* he?

He debated endlessly. If he left, he'd be giving up all the benefits—a plot of land, a cheap home loan, a college education, and, perhaps most important of all, a place in San Cuervo. If he left, he'd be no one, nowhere, and he'd always be looking over his shoulder for the Crow.

Joe jabbed the pause button. "Hello? You there, Mary?"

"I knew I shouldn't have slept with you on your birthday. My sister was right."

"Your sister's so blonde she doesn't even get blonde jokes."

"That's not funny."

"I know. It's a serious condition. She should really see someone."

"Shut up, Joe. Are you coming over or not?"

"To do what?"

She scoffed. "What do you think?"

Joe knew: make babies. And there was a part of him that wanted to do just that, an aching part that said, *If you die tomorrow, leave something behind.* Joe ignored it. To impregnate Mary, even symbolically, would be to admit that he might die tomorrow night, and Joe wasn't willing to do that.

And what if Mary had a son? A boy who would one day be eighteen?

"I don't know," he said. "I have a big day tomorrow."

"A big day?" Her voice spiked, loud and harsh in his ear. "A big fucking day?"

"Yes. And I have a lot to think about, so if you don't mind..."

Silence. Then she whispered, "I think I know what this is about."

"Enlighten me."

"You're scared."

"Am not."

But he was, even though scared was too small a word to describe it.

"It's okay if you are. Maybe I can make you feel better."

This again. "I don't want to give up anything. I like everything I have."

Another long silence, punctuated by a strange clicking on the line.

"Hello?" Joe asked.

"You shouldn't talk like that," she said finally. "It's blasphemy."

"Like what? Like the Crow's bullshit? Like he doesn't protect us. I mean, what is he even protecting us *from*? And why should I have to give up something? It makes no sense."

"You really shouldn't talk like that. I'm going to hang up."

"Don't be silly," he said. But she was already gone.

They had been raised not to question the Crow or His Harvest, not to question Old Man Marshall's Scarecrow farm or his exclusive wholeness, to accept that every boy in San Cuervo has something to give, something the Crow needs to go on living, and that it's not their place to question His will. The Crow protects San Cuervo and San Cuervo protects the Crow. All men are called to Give. But they're comforted by the fact that the Crow only kills when it's absolutely necessary, when He needs a new heart or a new liver or a new brain. And if you're lucky enough to provide the Crow with one of these essential organs, your soul is fast-tracked to Heaven, to Joy Beyond Reckoning, Forever. And a stone is added to the Mound for you.

You may have been dismembered, but you are remembered.

The Crow has been alive a long time, longer than San Cuervo.

Back when the Mound Builders lived here, and even before. Long before.

Parts of Him failed, every year. He had to keep replacing parts to stay alive.

And if He were to die, you don't even want to know what might happen.

But, when you're a kid, eighteen seems like it will never come. And so you go on living, and you never question the will of the Crow, and you know that your own father went through it—he's missing all the toes on his left foot—and you know that you will someday proudly show your own sons your own wounds, those gleaming badges that say, *I did my part. I am a man.*

But then eighteen comes. Then it's real.

Then you know, on Halloween, you'll have to sneak into Old Man Marshall's farm with the other eighteeners, steal enough Scarecrow to roll a joint with the dried herbs, and pass it in a circle, inhaling deeply until everyone feels the effects.

How do you know when you feel the effects?

You'll know, they say. You'll know.

After Joe hung up the phone, he went back to Call of Duty. The pixilated unreality of the video game warfare calmed him. A night with Mary, as good as it might feel, would be too real.

He had less than twenty-four hours until the Harvest began.

Halloween came like it always did. A black cat slinking out of the darkness. All over town, chimneys blasted plumes of smoke like gigantic cigarettes into the sky where it joined the dark clouds, forming a layer of grunge that threatened to blot out the weak, pumpkin-colored autumn sun. The chill air was ripe with rotting apples. Jack-o'-lanterns stood sentry on every porch with geometric eyes and serrated grins.

Joe walked. He wasn't sure how far, or for how long. It was morning. In five or six hours, the street would fill with ghouls and goblins and mummies and demons. Hunger gnawed at him, and he wished for a fun-sized Snickers. But he was far too old for trick-or-treating.

The streets were lined with black flags, billowing in the October wind. Many were faded from repeated use. It looked like a twisted version of Independence Day. All the townspeople

Joe passed wore tiny black ribbons on their lapels in honor of the Harvest.

Joe wasn't sure where he was going until he got there. The Memorial Mound. It was in a clearing in the woods and had been there for thousands of years. The residents of San Cuervo still added stones to it to mark the fallen. Joe stood in the dusty shade of the ancient redwoods, some of which were younger than the Mound, and tried to imagine his parents heaving a stone of remembrance onto the sacred monument after he was gone. He couldn't picture it.

He headed home to spend some time with his mom and sister, Sally. He didn't expect to see his father that night. Some fathers built their entire lives around being proud of their Harvest sacrifices. Others barely mentioned their eighteenth years. Joe's father was one of the latter.

When Joe got home, he stepped into the kitchen, stared at his mother for a long time, then embraced her and cried against her chest like the child he still was.

The day faded, another rusted leaf on an autumn tree. Sally transformed into a princess. While Joe's father was still at work, his mother took her trick-or-treating.

When they left, Sally kissed Joe on the cheek. "I'll save my Snickers for you."

The kid has no clue, Joe thought. *No clue.*

His mother pulled him into a too-tight hug. Tears filled her eyes.

"Come home, damn it," she whispered. "You come home tonight."

Then the princess and her chaperone queen departed.

When night had fallen, Joe contemplated running again.

If he was going to do it, he had to do it now. He went upstairs and felt the weight of his suitcase in his hand, but he couldn't find it in his heart to leave San Cuervo behind. If he could just get through this night, the rest of his life would be easy, he told himself. He took a deep breath, stuffed the suitcase back under his bed, hopped on his bike, and rode out to Old Man Marshall's farm.

Kyle and Derek were already waiting for him there. They were the other eighteeners this year. Kyle was an acquaintance at best. Derek may as well have been an enemy. He used to bully Joe back in grade school until he discovered girls. Joe still suffered PTSD from third grade.

Their parents knew that Joe, Kyle, and Derek would all be eighteen the same year, and therefore would all face the Crow together. They arranged play dates when the boys were still in diapers. But it didn't stick. If anything, the boys made a conscious effort *not* to be friends.

The truth was, Joe couldn't see Kyle or Derek without thinking about the Crow, without thinking about that distant, then not-so-distant, now here, night when they would sacrifice pieces of themselves.

They weren't dressed up for Halloween. They had no need for costumes this year.

"We were starting to think you weren't gonna come," Derek said.

Joe flipped him off. The three boys laughed nervously, partly because Joe might be losing that very finger before the night was over.

Derek pointed at the scarecrow, which was staked in the center of Sam Marshall's field. "We gonna do this or not?"

"Who's going first?" Kyle asked.

"You," Derek said, and pushed him into the field. Kyle stumbled but didn't fall.

"Hell no," Kyle said. "I'm not going until you guys come too."

"Fine." Derek sighed. "Let's go."

He grabbed Joe by the arm and led him into the field. Joe wanted to run more than anything. And he knew the other boys did too. But none of them ran. They kept inching forward, toward their shared fate.

They finally reached the scarecrow. It stared blankly down at them.

"What now?" Kyle asked.

"We get stoned on Scarecrow," Derek said. "I heard it's like pot, only stronger."

"Stronger?" Kyle asked.

"Sure. My dad said, when he did it, before the...Crow came, it was the best feeling in his life. What do you guys say we take a little for ourselves, you know, for later?"

"No," Joe said.

He'd heard the story. It was actually a parable for the way of the Crow—take only what you need. Back in the sixties, some boys managed to smuggle a little baggie of the Scarecrow out. When their Harvest wounds had healed, they decided to smoke some of it recreationally, and the Crow came back to finish them off. He made an example of them—three boys, swinging from the Main Street stoplight in the center of town. And at their feet, the stolen Scarecrow, stomped into the asphalt.

"Fine," Derek said. "Let's just get this over with."

He took a small handful of the herbs from the scarecrow's chest and sat cross-legged in the field. Joe and Kyle sat with him, watching him grind the Scarecrow to a fine powder between his fingers, line it up on a rolling paper, lick it, then roll a perfect Scarecrow joint. He made it look easy. He'd clearly been practicing.

"Who wants the first hit?" Derek said, smiling. Was he actually enjoying this?

When Joe and Kyle said nothing, Derek shrugged, flicked a lighter, and lit the joint. The burning herb had a sour reek. A ghostly cherry hovered in front of Derek's face. He held a deep hit in and exhaled with a coughing fit so violent tears streamed down his face.

His coughing morphed into laughter. "Smooth," he said, and took another hit.

He passed the joint to Kyle, who inhaled deeply and coughed just as Derek had.

Then Kyle passed it to Joe. He brought it to his lips. The paper was moist with saliva. The scent was intoxicating, almost toxic. He felt lightheaded just smelling the smoke.

"What are you waiting for?" Derek asked.

Joe closed his lips around the joint and inhaled slowly. The smoke burned his throat and singed his lungs. He held it in as long as he could and then coughed up a cloud of dark mist. He immediately felt like he was going to lose consciousness. He shut his heavy eyes.

"Hey," Derek said. "Pass that over here."

He held out the joint. Derek snatched if from him.

Joe opened his eyes and...everything was the same. The scarecrow still leered down at him. The three boys still sat cross-legged in the field. Derek passed the joint back to Kyle.

"You guys feel anything yet?" Derek asked.

Joe couldn't speak for the others—hell, he couldn't even speak—but he felt it.

His entire being was a slowly opening eye.

He stood. They all did.

They surrounded the scarecrow and held hands. Derek's hands were chubby and clammy. Kyle's were thin and calloused. Why the hell were they holding hands? They never would have, in normal, sober life. But right now, it felt natural, almost inevitable.

They began to hum, three distinct notes, a minor chord.

The harmony rose, clashed. Overtones rang out.

Joe could see the sound, now. An orange fog, rising, darkening.

Their mouths gaped and tones poured from them like pipes on a vast organ.

The chord changed.

The scarecrow was lost in the darkness of the music they made. They could no longer see its obscure face. Soon, they surrounded nothing but the ominous sound.

And now there was a fourth note in their harmony, a complex, jangling chord.

The boys closed their eyes. They stopped singing.

One note continued ringing out, growing, pulsing.

A wavering, sour, out-of-tune note. Vomit from the belly of jazz.

Joe opened his eyes.

Standing in the center of their circle, where the scarecrow was once staked—the Crow. His massive body was covered in a cloak of black feathers like a kind of armor. The 'feathers' looked hard, scaly. Beneath, He was a hideous, disfigured thing, made of the rotting parts of the men of San Cuervo. All those patched-together pieces of skin, each a slightly different hue, gave His body beneath the armor the look of desert camouflage. He crouched and tucked His wings behind him. His talons scratched at the earth. He had a black beak protruding from the mask on His face, like a plague doctor in old paintings Joe had seen in History class.

The Crow stopped singing.

All was silent.

The Scarecrow joint smoldered fragrantly nearby, forgotten in the grass.

Joe saw something glinting in the Crow's...hand? Claw? Was He a bird or a man? It was hard to tell. An old god, perhaps. A little bit of each. But He had hands. And in one of His hands, He held a hunting knife with a ten-inch blade.

He lunged for Kyle, grabbed his arm, brought the blade down swiftly, and cut off Kyle's hand at the wrist. A jet of black blood erupted from the stump. Derek screamed. The Crow held up the severed hand in the moonlight, studied it, and stashed it away in His feathery coat. Kyle fell to the ground, howling and clutching his wrist.

Derek turned to run. He made it about ten steps before the Crow lifted off the ground, spread His enormous wings, and reached Derek in one horrifying leap. He pinned Derek down, and—using His hands that weren't quite claws, His claws that weren't quite hands—He popped out both of Derek's eyeballs, admired them, and tucked them away in His plumage.

Derek remained on the ground, sobbing blood from cavernous sockets.

Joe held his ground, watching the dark shape of the Crow lurch toward him, watching the Crow's bloody blade glisten in the pallid moonlight. He walked up to Joe, deliberately, and stood before him, looking him up and down as if deciding which piece to harvest first.

Joe closed his eyes.

He felt the blade plunge deep into his chest, splitting him open.

He felt a hand root around inside his chest cavity.

He felt his heart being ripped from his body, heard the wet snap.

His eyes opened and he watched, curiously detached, as the Crow held up his heart and examined it in the bone-colored light of the Halloween moon.

Guess I'm one of the lucky ones, Joe thought. *One of the remembered ones.*

He closed his eyes.

When he opened them, he'd see Heaven.

He just knew he would.

Old Man Marshall surveyed his field on the morning of November first, shaking his head.

Lots of blood, but there always was. Looked like a morning-after battlefield.

And this time, damn it, a body.

There had been three. Two of them must have made their way off the farm. But one... One would be staying to fertilize next year's crop.

He took down the scarecrow and emptied it of its stuffing. Tonight, after San Cuervo had gone to sleep, he'd burn what was left of his crop in a bonfire. He wouldn't dare smoke the stuff himself, and he didn't trust having it on hand. The local boys were curious about his plants, and rightly so. He didn't want them jumping the gun and smoking Scarecrow before their eighteenth birthdays. Didn't want to find out what'd happen if the Crow caught wind of it.

The boy's body left a trail of gore as Sam Marshall dragged it across the fallow field and into the latticework enclosure where he grew the Scarecrow.

Then, the old man—still whole, praise the Crow—began to dig.

BRINGING IN THE MAY

By Stephanie Ellis

The doors opened and Nell's heart sank. For once, the Friday night/Saturday morning shift had delivered half the usual admissions of the drunk and the drugged. The A&E ward felt almost peaceful. She did not need this.

Liam appeared at her shoulder. "I'll see to these. Go grab yourself a coffee. Haven't seen you take a break yet."

"Thanks," said Nell, grateful. "Next time I volunteer to do a double shift, please stop me."

"I tried. Remember?"

He had, and she hadn't listened, aware of how short-staffed they were, of the half-empty bottles in her flat, of the tears they failed to drown. Home alone was not a good place to be. It held too much grief. And a grief numbed by alcohol had caused her to make some horrendous mistakes on duty.

Nell's life was in limbo whilst the world moved on. The police had closed the case and her sister had been consigned to the statistics. Dead, they said. They had a confession; they didn't need the body. But she did.

Connie was still out there, somewhere.

Nell watched Liam guide the new admission to a cubicle,

but instead of disappearing to the staffroom, she made her way to a nearby vending machine where the man's companion was pushing coins in the slot. It was Shawn, one of the few genuinely caring people left in the community, a tireless campaigner for the down and outs, the have-nots of Winchester. He stood, with a couple of carrier bags at his feet, sipping a coffee, waiting for her.

"Evening, Nell. Quiet night tonight?"

He smelt of the city, of night air and booze and sweat, odors transferred from those he literally lifted off the pavement.

"Yeah, makes a change." She didn't want small talk. "Did you—?"

"Yes. It's all done. Took her clothes round to the shelter. Furniture and stuff have all gone to Oxfam. Anything I wasn't sure of, a few books, photo albums, personal stuff, you know? Is here."

Nell looked down at the remnants of her sister's life. "Thank you. I owe you."

With the verdict had come her sister's landlord's demand to empty the flat so he could relet it. He didn't want to be insensitive, he'd said, but he was losing money. Nell couldn't face going there and Shawn had offered, and she trusted him.

He studied her carefully. "You look exhausted. You should really take a holiday. Aren't you due some time off?"

"I don't think I could face it. All those people enjoying themselves whilst Connie is—" She stopped, unable to bear the sympathy in his eyes.

"Time away from here though. That would be a good thing, surely? Somewhere out in the countryside. Fresh air, peace and quiet."

Nell laughed. "On my wages? Only the rich can afford a holiday in this country."

"Or those with connections," said Shawn, smirking.

"Huh?"

"Toby's cottage, remember? The village is only a few miles

away, but it's a different world!"

A memory stirred. "Oh, I know the one! Connie spent some time there the year before... before... she disappeared. She came back raving about the place. Went on a real nature kick." Nell suppressed a sob with difficulty.

"Toby told me to tell you it's there for you, if you'd like to go. Free gratis. Unless the association is too painful?"

She thought for a moment, then decided. "No. It was a place she was happy. I think I'd like to visit, if that's okay?"

"Leave it with me," said Shawn.

Her sister's belongings sat on the passenger seat. They had remained untouched in her flat, until today. It felt right to Nell that she should finally go through these in a place her sister had been happy.

Despite it being a Saturday morning, the roads were surprisingly quiet, and it was easy to follow Shawn's directions. Kinlet did not appear on Google Maps—too inconsequential, he'd said, and her Sat Nav seemed to agree.

Much of the route was recognizable, until she pulled off the main road and onto a narrow lane. Unable to see round the bends, and with hedges high and rampant with fresh spring growth, Nell slowed right down, let the car crawl along, making mental notes of the few passing places on the way. Her luck held, however, and soon the lane widened out at a signpost which proclaimed Kinlet only two miles away.

The sun shone, the skies remained cloudless and the roads empty. Nell allowed herself to relax.

Oleander Cottage was the first house after the village sign, and one of only a handful of houses on the approach. Shawn had said Kinlet consisted of a couple of dozen dwellings, yet somehow maintained a pub, a small grocers and a craft-and-coffee shop. A hit with tourists apparently, although nothing could be found on TripAdvisor. Distractions, should she need it.

Parking up in the drive, Nell allowed herself a minute to take in the house. It was just like the photo Connie had shown her and, for a moment, it was as if her sister was nearby. The scent of spring drifted through her open window. Early blooming roses grew along the pathway, whilst late daffodils remained to add a splash of yellow.

She stretched and took a deep breath, picked up the bags—including her sister's—and made her way up the path. A frothy garland of yellow flowers hung on the front door. She bent to sniff them, but pulled back at the musty aroma which stung her eyes and made her vision swim.

The image of flowers faded and all she could see were rotting twigs and mildewed leaves, shriveled moss and decaying petals. A movement caught her eye and closer inspection revealed a beetle. It paused its work and seemed to stare at her. Nell shook her head and the beetle vanished, the garland reappearing as it had done at first sight, the bouquet too, a reflection of that in the garden.

Shaken by this sudden apparition, Nell headed inside. Stress and exhaustion had a lot to answer for.

The interior was an olde worlde delight. She recalled Connie crowing about the beams and the open hearth, the aga and the traditionally styled kitchen. A box of groceries sat on the table and the note, from the ever-solicitous Shawn, told her there was plenty in the fridge too. She need do nothing but enjoy her break.

Nell put Connie's bags beside the box and made her way up to the bedroom. The sight of the bed brought on a yawn. Without another thought, she kicked off her shoes and lay down. She was asleep in seconds.

It was the distant chime of a church bell that eventually

woke Nell. She counted. One, two, three o'clock. She'd slept five solid hours. Not a lot by most people's standards, but for her such an unbroken spell was unheard of in recent times.

Her thoughts turned to her sister's bags, waiting downstairs. Their presence called her, and Nell knew it was time.

Reluctantly, she went to the kitchen and started to investigate. One carrier contained photo albums, pictures of them growing up, of family and friends. The last, smaller album contained a picture of Oleander Cottage and nothing else, although from the look of it, there had been others before they'd been removed.

Nell put it aside and picked up a book. *Celtic Pagan Beliefs*. She grinned, remembering this one. Connie had really got into it, the ancient worship of the triple goddess, the representation of Mother Nature. She'd even set up her own shrine to 'the Mother'.

Some had mocked her sister, but not Nell. She had seen how these practices, archaic as they were, had given her a sense of peace. And she had envied her that.

"You should try it," had said Connie. "It really shows you how things are."

And she nearly had, had just started to read the books Connie recommended, when her sister disappeared. Perhaps she should try again. It would be a way of keeping her sister with her.

The second bag contained a couple of battered cuddly toys, treasured relics of childhood, the last links to their parents, and a shoebox.

Nell lifted the box lid. Scraps of paper, letters, tickets and keyrings jostled messily against each other, but nestled on top, cradled by the contents, lay a small doll. Palm-sized, it was a hideous object.

Raising it up to get a better look, she noted the head was a bird's skull, giving it the appearance of a plague doctor; the clothes, a tattered robe of patchwork, a deep, cowled hood pulled over empty eyes. Unwillingly, she pushed a sleeve back and discovered tiny bones formed the hand and arm, likewise the other limbs and trunk.

Gruesome as it was, she had to admit some skill had gone into its making. Connie loved poking about in craft shops and finding weird little artefacts. This one was typical of her sister's taste.

Nell placed the figure on a shelf, thinking about Kinlet's craft shop. It probably came from there. Handling the skeletal doll brought with it an uncomfortable sensation, a claustrophobic reminder of the nearness of the dead to the living. She needed fresh air.

She didn't want to go into the village. Mixing with people was not part of her plan just yet. Instead, she walked to the back of the garden where she'd spotted a small gate. It led out onto a track which wound its way up a gentle slope behind the house. An old, wooden sign indicated a public footpath.

Reassured she wasn't trespassing, Nell set off along the track, pausing every now and then to stop and look back, take in the view of the countryside as the village and its environs unfolded before her. When she reached the top, she was able to see that Kinlet occupied a small dip in a narrow valley. It carried a strangely isolated air about it.

Shrugging off the sensation, Nell crested the hill and found herself in the presence of a group of standing stones. They were exactly as Connie had described.

In the center of a slight depression stood two megaliths, with a third boulder placed across the top to create a trilithon, reminding her of Stonehenge. Two other stones stood either side, lined up with the gap between the two central stones. Nell looked around for an English Heritage information board. Even in the middle of nowhere, they could usually be found, imparting the history of the area in which they were situated.

Here, there was nothing.

Nell went up to the nearest stone, which towered over her. Standing in front of it, she looked directly through the portal at its twin and at that moment, her sister's face came back to her, reigniting her sense of loss. At the same time, she felt more connected to her absent sibling than she had ever done.

It was a strange duality, presence and absence in one place. The grass at her feet and through the portal was well-trodden.

"You walked through here, didn't you, Connie?" A breeze brushed her cheek in answer. "I'll come back," she said. "I know you're here somewhere. I'll find you."

A peace she had not felt for a long time settled over her as she headed down the hill, the bells chiming five as she opened the back door, her thoughts turning to food.

A small tub on the top shelf of the fridge appeared to hold a casserole. 'Freshly made, Sue x', said the label. Sue was the cook at the homeless shelter.

"Bless you, Sue," Nell murmured, and put the tub in the microwave.

Taking a plate from the nearby cupboard, she turned, and almost dropped it. The doll, which she had tucked away on a shelf, was sat in the middle of the table, a shriveled witch, glaring at her.

Suddenly, her vision shifted and the room changed, became a broken structure of cracked plaster and rotting beams, shattered windows and filthy surfaces. She gripped the plate tightly and closed her eyes, counting to ten, certain that like before, the illusion would pass. Thankfully, it did.

Shaken, Nell grabbed a chair and sat down, closing and re-opening her eyes a number of times to see if it happened again. It did not. The cottage had returned to its pristine image, and the doll had vanished.

When the microwave pinged, she ignored it, dwelling on the hallucinations and dizzy spells. It could be stress, but the nurse in her told her a checkup wouldn't hurt. She would book an appointment when she got back home.

Having made the decision, Nell relaxed and took out her meal from the microwave. Sue had outdone herself as usual, but Nell kept her eyes closed as she ate. She didn't want to see her food turn into something else.

When her fork was unable to find any more food, she opened her eyes—and immediately cursed herself. The doll was back, the air shimmered, and maggots crawled across the table, wriggling over her empty plate.

She squeezed her eyes shut again, counted to twenty this time, begged for everything to be normal. Taking a deep breath, and still shaking, she looked. Normality had returned. Nell retreated to the sitting room, annoyed now there was no television to divert her.

Her recent sense of peace had proved miserably temporary.

The sofa sat directly opposite the open fireplace. Logs had been laid ready, but it was too warm at the moment for a fire. Above the mantelpiece was an old painting, of the stones and a crowd of people, shadows at its edges. A young woman was facing the viewer from the other side of the stone doorway. She was holding out her hands. The resemblance to Connie was uncanny.

Beneath the hanging stone, a fire burned. The feeling of connection to her sister—and to the henge—strengthened.

"What happened to you, Sis?" she wondered aloud. "You said there were hidden layers in the natural world, places only a few could go. Is that where you went?"

Silence was her answer. Had she honestly expected a reply from Connie? But her sister had felt so present, so close. Nell stretched out on the sofa and stared at the painting, focusing on the fire which, like its counterpart in reality, seemed to have the ability to hypnotize. The world receded as her eyelids drooped, and it wasn't long before she was fast asleep, her sister a shadow in her dreams.

The cold light of dawn woke Nell this time. Groaning at the ache in her body, she rose from the sofa and made her way into the kitchen, desperate for water to relieve her dry throat. Nell downed two glasses before she headed to the shower and a change of clothes. Outside, the day promised fair. With a last look at the painting, she slipped Connie's book in her backpack and headed up the hill. The stones were calling.

As she looked down on the village, she could see people starting to move, a few already gathered by the maypole.

"Should've moved here, Connie," said Nell. "I'd've joined you."

And she meant it. Kinlet felt like the haven she'd longed for. She settled herself at the base of a stone and leaned back against its surface. The sun had warmed it already. For the next two hours, she buried herself in the ancient ways of the Celts.

"I think they treated Mother Nature better than we ever have," said Nell, continuing her habit of talking to Connie as if she was there. The old ways seemed so simple. "I wonder if you ever got to see her?"

Connie had often mentioned her as a tangible entity, and Toby, Shawn's co-worker amongst the homeless, had been of the same mindset.

"I used to tease the pair of you that you were starting a cult. Better get going though, see what the villagers get up to, see if they do it 'right', for you. See you later, Connie."

Her sister was there, she knew it. When the time was right, she would show herself and Nell could lay her ghost to rest.

She reached the cottage just as Shawn walked up the pathway.

"Where've you been?"

"Up to the stones, to see Connie. Spent some time talking to her. She's there, I know it."

A shadow passed over his face. "Nell, I know you've been under some strain recently. I think—"

"She's doing exactly the right thing." It was Toby. She hadn't noticed his arrival. "The May is a time of both death and rebirth and the spirits are close to us. Especially in the places they were happy."

Shawn looked at Toby. "Forgot you and Connie were into that Beltane nonsense."

"Might be nonsense to you," said Toby. "But it keeps me sane—and alive. And you call it nonsense, yet the whole village puts on a show, the maypole, the fire."

"Good for business," said Shawn. "A bit of theatrics for YouTube, put us on the map."

It sounded like an old argument between them. "Nature viewed through a screen is no experience."

"The village needs the income to survive."

Toby shook his head. "No. I've told you. Return to the old ways—properly—and you won't have to worry again.

"You're as bad as Nick!"

"Your brother has sense," retorted Toby. "You should follow his lead."

The two had almost forgotten Nell as they bickered their way into the village, until the greetings of those out and about distracted them.

Toby gazed across the Maypole. "This is all pretense," he said to Nell, "but later, you'll see the true meaning of the May."

Shawn rolled his eyes, then nudged her. "There's my brother Nick."

Nell turned to see Shawn's double appear at the pub door. "I can see the resemblance. You're not twins, are you?"

Nick laughed at her words. "Nah, he's my baby brother. Got a year or two on him. Welcome to our humble village, by the way. Come on in and try what we have to offer."

"Sorry," said Nell, shaking her head. "Unless it's a soft drink. I'm on a bit of a health kick."

She had promised herself not to touch another drop whilst on holiday.

"Ah, the bane of modern life," said Nick, seemingly disapproving. "We have some lovely apple punch though. Not a whiff of alcohol in it. I'll go and get some and we can take it over to the green. Kids are about to start dancing. You don't want to miss that."

"He means they usually tie themselves in knots—literally. It is quite funny."

"None of that, Shawn," said a woman, passing by with a little girl in tow. "They'll get it right this year."

The child giggled and waved at Shawn who winked in return.

"Here you go." Nick returned to her side and handed over a glass of light gold liquid.

She sipped it carefully and it slithered down her throat. "Oh, that is good!"

The sound of strings tuning broke into their conversation, and Nell allowed the brothers to lead her across to the maypole. Toby had vanished. The music started and the children, by now positioned and holding their ribbons, began to dance. Slowly at first, they wove in and out without a fault. Then the music became faster, the children spinning in front of her, faster still, so it became a blur, and then it happened.

Color leached from her sight, as if the world in front of her was thinning, with no more substance than a piece of gauze. The figures continued to swirl against this, distorting the world further, but not blocking the sight of something lurking in the darkness beyond. A face gradually emerged, eyes piercing the veil to look straight at her—Connie.

Nell swayed and dropped her glass.

Shawn took her arm and steadied her. "Nell? You alright? Come over here."

He led her to a nearby bench and Nick offered her another drink.

Embarrassment flushed her face. "Sorry. I'm fine, honestly. Had a bit of a dizzy spell, that's all."

"Food," said Nick. "That's what you need. Health kick, my eye. You need a bit of meat on your bones and I've just the thing. Won't be a sec."

"It's a bit early, isn't it?" Yet as she spoke, the bells chimed noon. That couldn't be! The children couldn't have been dancing for two hours. She took a deep breath, managed to hold herself together. "Thank you. That's very kind."

Nick delivered on his promise. "Can't go wrong with a homemade cottage pie." He looked at her. "You're not one of them vegetarians, are you?"

She shook her head and accepted the plate. His smile at her response told him she'd gone up in his estimation.

They sat at a picnic table, eating and quietly chatting. Mostly Nick and Shawn, telling stories of the village, introducing locals as they stopped to say hello, recounting childhood shenanigans whilst Nell listened and allowed her mind and body to quieten. Every now and then, she would spot Toby moving amongst the villagers, whispering in their ears. Occasionally, he would look her way and smile.

Her newly regained sense of peace was shattered however, when she reached into her bag for a tissue. She felt cold bone beneath her fingers and froze. Part of her wanted to crush the thing, but something told her it would return yet again to haunt her.

She should give it to Shawn. He could take it away. Nell pulled out the small doll and placed it on the table between the two men. They fell quiet.

"Connie's May Doll," said Shawn, picking it up. "I remember her getting it from the shop. Quite taken with it, she was, despite its appearance. These are one of the traditions I wish they'd left dead and buried. A lot of people feel the same. Have you seen them in the wreaths on the doors round here? Ugh."

"Why do they make them if so many dislike them?"

"Oh, it's one of Toby's special requests, and it's a way of keeping him quiet. They're all burned in the bonfire at the end of the day. According to Toby, it's supposed to represent the death of the Crone and the rebirth of the Maid. The ones in the Craft Shop aren't for burning though. They're 'quirky' souvenirs for folk to take away with them."

Nell laughed. "If this wasn't Connie's, I'd actually say the flames would be welcome to it." She stifled a yawn. The meal had made her feel drowsy. "Hope you don't mind, but I think I need to go and lie down for a bit. All this fresh air has caught up with me! I'll be alright," she added, as Shawn rose to accompany her.

"Make sure you come back for the bonfire," said Nick. "It's quite something."

She nodded and returned to the cottage, where she proceeded to sleep the rest of the day away. Her time with the stones had soothed her mind. She had enjoyed the morning, watching the maypole dancers, browsing in the craft shops, talking to a few of the locals. They had been welcoming, especially when they discovered she was Connie's sister.

Her funny turn was a distant memory, easily dismissed as her body telling her it needed rest. She was looking forward to the bonfire Nick had mentioned. And perhaps Toby would talk of his beliefs with her, as he had done with Connie. Shawn had already made his disapproval clear, but it didn't matter.

Nell felt as if her life had begun again, and the path her sister had taken was one she was increasingly drawn to.

When she awoke, it was to a room blanketed by darkness. Her watch revealed the time to be 9.30. It wouldn't be long until they lit the fire, and she didn't want to miss talking to Toby again. Stepping out into the cool night air, she noted the moon, fat and full, shining down on the village. The lane was quiet and there were no lights in nearby windows. It didn't unnerve her, as she had been told pretty much the whole community attended the event.

Nell paused at her nearest neighbor's gate and looked at the garland still adorning it. The doll which had previously sat in its center had gone. Gathered at Toby's insistence, no doubt.

By now, she had reached the middle of the village, but the silence remained absolute. No lights in the small enclave of buildings, and the pub proclaimed itself closed. All signs of the morning's festivities had vanished. Nell struggled to remember what Shawn had said about the bonfire. Where had he said to go?

She gazed around, mind blank, until she noticed a flicker from the hillside. The stones. That was it!

She started to head back towards the cottage, intending to take the track from her garden, when a giggle caught her ear and the nearby hedgerow stirred. She could see a shadowy path, barely lit by the streetlight. A footpath sign included an image of the stones. There was no need to trek all the way back up the lane. She set off along the path without another thought, pleased to discover the track was relatively wide and well-maintained.

Someone started to sing. A child from the sound of it. The familiar words made her smile, sent her back to her own childhood.

"Here we come gathering nuts in May, nuts in May, nuts in May,

Here we come gathering nuts in May, so early in the morning."

Nell started to quietly sing along and then stopped. Her invisible companion was singing different words.

"Here we come gathering blood in May, blood in May, blood in May

Here we come gathering for Mother's Day, so early in the morning."

Another giggle, and a rustle up ahead. A breeze stirred the overhanging branches, sending them reaching out for her. Nell ducked and carried on.

"Who will we take for meat in May, meat in May, meat in May

Who will we take for Mother's Day, so early in the morning."

The voice was no longer sweet and innocent. Its tone had

deepened into a growl, and another had joined in to create an unnerving duet.

An owl hooted and shadows flew out overhead, causing her to jump. Nell considered returning to her cottage, but the villagers had been so welcoming, had insisted she join in their celebrations, so she continued on, trying not to listen to her tormentors up ahead.

She stopped for a moment, hoping to increase the gap between herself and the little monsters. When she discovered who their parents were, she would have words.

As she looked around, she noticed a May Doll sat astride the hedge on her left. It was looking right at her. Nell moved away swiftly, stopping in her tracks when the song became louder, indicating she was too close. And there sat another doll. Now she was walking quickly, eyes fixed on the hedgerow running alongside the track, taking in figure after hideous figure.

All of them watching her.

"We will have Nell to feed the fire in May, fire in May, fire in May

We will have her kindling for Mother's Day, so early in the morning."

The dolls were no longer just watching her; their bony beaks had opened, and their terrible voices added to those she had followed. Nell felt sick. She had slept but not eaten since lunchtime. Hunger was making her see things, that was all.

And then she was out in the open.

"Nell!"

At the sound of Shawn's familiar voice, Nell turned gratefully towards him. Moving quickly to put the sight of the dolls behind her, she crested the hill and dashed into the comforting light of the fire blazing between the megaliths. Shawn was nowhere to be seen. There was no one there at all.

"Who will you have to cut her in May, cut her in May, cut her in May,

Who will you have cut for Mother's Day, so early in the morning."

More voices and Nell turned to see a crowd of robed figures move to the edge of the circle, fanning out so she became imprisoned in their midst. Her mind was racing, one side insisting the dolls had somehow come to life, become giants. The logical part said it was the villagers, dressed up to frighten her.

One left the crowd and joined her in the circle. Despite not seeing his face, from his build, from his voice when he spoke, from the eyes she could just make out behind the skull mask, she could tell it was Toby.

"Toby! What—?"

He raised his fingers to his lips and she obediently fell quiet.

"Friends, welcome to the Mother's hearth. She has invited us here, as she has done for centuries, to receive our offerings, in return for which, she has given us good harvests and good health."

One or two figures moved round the circle handing out drinks, before entering the circle and giving the last to Toby and Nell. She remembered he had told her he would show her the truth of the May. Feeling somewhat reassured, she accepted the tumbler.

Toby raised his glass in a toast. "To the May and to the Mother."

"To the May and the Mother," responded the crowd, draining their glasses.

He looked at her. "Drink."

Nell took a sip and almost spat it out. It tasted bitter. Something swam on the surface. Her stomach heaved as she saw a worm-like creature wriggling amongst the bubbles. It recalled the maggots on her plate.

"Drink," repeated Toby.

She prayed this was no more than some jazzed-up version

of mezcal or tequila or whatever it was that included beetle larvae as a bonus. The movement of the worm in her drink, however, seemed to indicate something else.

"All of it," he added, so she was in no doubt.

Closing her eyes and trying to switch off all senses, she drank it down. To her surprise, the bitterness had vanished, replaced by a slight sweetness and an earthy malt flavor that was not unpleasant. As soon as her glass was empty, everyone cheered and moved forward, congratulating her drinking the offering.

Toby had removed his mask, but the crowd retained theirs. They felt different. Strangers.

Toby seemed to read her mind. "Not strangers, your new family."

"Where's Shawn? Nick? The villagers?"

"Where they should be," said Toby, leading her the short way to the brow of the hill. "Down there, playing with fire."

Nell could see flames from below. A bonfire had been lit on the village green. But it hadn't been there earlier, nor had anyone else.

She thought of her journey up the hill. "The dolls. Were they a test?"

He took her arm and gently guided her back into the circle. "Look around," he said. "Tell me what you see."

She looked and realized that those who had watched her progress along the track now stood before her, albeit grown.

"They are part of the hidden world," continued Toby. "The world your sister was able to enter."

"Connie? Connie's here?" She'd been right about the connection, she'd felt her, could feel her now, somewhere close by.

"Yes," said Toby, "but it's for you to find her. She's waiting."

Nell spun round, could see nothing except the fire in front of her. It had dropped. Nell moved closer. There was something through the stone portal, a figure in shadow, a familiar shape, voice.

"Come gather with me, the nuts in May, the nuts in May, the nuts in May

Come join me and the Mother, and feed the May, early in the morning."

Connie!

Another step closer to the fire.

"Nell."

"Do you see her, Toby?" she cried. "Do you see Connie?"

"I see her, Nell. Go to her and the Mother. They're waiting."

Without even thinking, Nell stepped into the fire. It roared up around her. There was no pain as she burned, eyes fixed on her sister, only the sensation of sloughing off a coat no longer required. And then the flames fell away and she stepped through the stones.

"You're getting better every time," said Shawn, "a master of your art. You made it look so easy with Connie, I couldn't believe you would get Nell to follow her sister."

"Theatrics," said Nick, joining them.

Toby sipped his beer. "But it worked, didn't it? We brought in the May for the Mother, and she will look after us, as always."

On the hill, a body smoldered in the ash.

THE TREASURE MAP INSIDE YOUR FACE IS COVERED IN BEES

By Patrick Barb

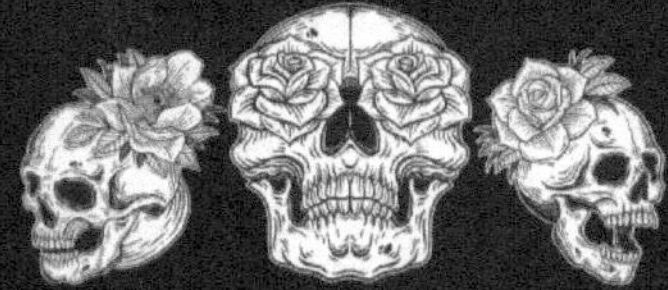

I wear your face to study your secrets up close. Blood and honey serve as adequate adhesives, keeping your distorted features in place over my own. I slather my tongue across one of the glossy 8x10s from my short-lived acting 'career'. I brought it here, to this soulless husk of a house, to remind you of what I looked like when we met. In the Poverty Row, noir-lit photograph, my black bowtie's loosened, ebony strands spooled from my throat to mar the white of my dress shirt. My gray-eyed stare and square chin could give Bogie a run for his money, if not for the long blonde hair cascading over my shoulders.

You remember that hair, don't you? You grabbed it in handfuls, as we navigated the waterbed in your old apartment. Were you pulling me in for a kiss—a kiss like this more two-dimensional one—or was I pulling you to me? We slammed together, faces colliding like shifting tectonic plates. Like aliens trying to reenact human affection observed from a clinical distance.

One time, rougher than the others, our front teeth shattered and we spat the fragments into each other's mouths. I told you weeks later I'd collected your feces, dug out the parts of my teeth you couldn't digest. But I lied.

I lied to you too often.

But my hair! I was talking about my hair, wasn't I?

It's gone now. Brushed out in chunks after the cancer diagnosis, the radiation, and the chemo. You sat at my bedside, not saying a word. Being there was enough. I know it sounds cliché, but it's the truth. It meant the world to me. And I know that sounds cliché too, but...

Even when the doctor gave me the all-clear and I rang the bell, giving the nurses and other walking corpses I once called my 'colleagues in death' a chance to cheer, a chance to experience anything for a moment aside from despair, you stood by and said nothing.

Will you say anything to me here while I'm holding your face?

Now I try to speak, and a fuzzy, black-and-yellow bumblebee presses its way through your lips, drowning my words in its droning buzz. Your cheeks sit askew over mine, but they bulge and hum with activity. Another bee emerges.

Then another and another.

Don't get up. Please. Sit in the corner, your now lidless eyes forever staring and your shallow breaths speckling the air with blood. Wait until I finish.

You were always good on that count.

I peel your face back and the bees go away. No traces of fuzzy, plump bodies or sharp, black stingers or tiny, translucent wings working overtime remain. Their honey pulls away some stray stubble across my chin, clouding the golden syrup with the short, black bristles of my 5 o'clock shadow.

I walk the short distance from the living room to the kitchen. Easy enough when there's no furniture in this model home, no sign of life except me, you with your bleeding, skinless head, the broken glass by the living room window, and those fleeing bumblebees.

I take off your face and wash it in the kitchen sink. I

might've been presumptuous earlier, putting your face on so fresh from its removal. It's time to wash away the blood and honey, scrub the stringy tendons of meat once connecting your long face, narrow eyes, and tall, tall ghost-white cheekbones to the muscle and bone you wear now.

It's like you've taken off one too many layers for this time of year, huh?

Don't worry. I'm careful not to wash too much. If I ever give it back, you'll still wear it without too much difference from how you appeared before.

The deep, blue-black lines on the inside resemble veins, but they come with a different purpose than carrying blood, pumping life through a body. I spread your face flat across the countertop, lift the hem of my shirt to dab away excess moisture.

I told your parents about you. About what you really are.

In all honesty, I never expected them to react the way they did. It shocked me when they went along with my plan, slipping crushed-up powders into your after-dinner coffee. A bit stronger than the Bailey's we'd spike our morning cups with on rainy days, when neither of us wanted to go to work, and after the layoffs, when there was no work to go to.

I didn't expect their help. And I certainly never expected what they did after I took your face. Old as they are—sorry, were—they climbed to the edge of the overpass across from here faster than I expected. But they sure fell as fast as you'd assume they'd fall.

What's wrong, no fairy dust to sprinkle on 'em so they'd fly?

Oh, stop! Don't moan at me like you ever cared. You were never their son. You were an imitation. An illusion.

This face in my hands, it's not even yours. You stole it. You stole it, and with it came the future of the baby it belonged to, who never grew into the child it belonged to, and never woke up confused and tired, always so tired, trying to understand the person it never became.

Please. Stop crying. Give me a moment to read the—what're these?—runes? Glyphs? You talk in your sleep, you know? You speak in the language of your people, even if you don't know what the words mean in the light of day, as you claim. In dreams, you know them well enough.

I'm a quick study. I've always had this knack for deciphering languages, cracking codes, and reading old maps. Must've got it from all those thick fantasy paperbacks I stayed up too late reading. The ones you called 'children's playthings'.

They taught me enough to bring me here.

At first, I thought you spoke in glossolalia. Some many-tongued speech of the angels, intoning the mysteries of the cosmos. But when I watched the home videos your mom put into the slideshow at the wedding reception, it clicked for me. Watching 'you' as this happy, rosy-cheeked cherubim one moment and then the pale, string-haired, gaunt shade the next, I understood where you'd come from. I knew what you were. What you are.

Under a canopy of trees in the dark forest abutting your parent's property, there wasn't enough light for roses to grow. So, as is the custom of your people, they snuck into that loving home, lifted the baby—the one meant to bear your name, your face, your life—up from his crib, and they made you wiggle and worm your way inside. You drew in your powers, your magic, your whatever-the-hell-you-want-to-call-it, and then, oh, you had to live a normal, boring life.

All this time, you lived a lie. Changeling. Double. Liar.

You kept your true self hidden. Hidden even from yourself.

I don't know what's worse. Taking away someone's life, for what, a lark? For a laugh shared in the throne room of Glory Anna or whatever name you shout when wet dreams twist your body under the covers, leaving our old sheets sticky, damp with your secrets and lies? Or is it worse to hide?

Consider yourself lucky all I took was your face. I could've carved the flesh from your back, dug around inside until I found your wings.

But I don't want to see how you could fly. I want your face. I want this map inside your face.

I know that's what I've found here. These old lines form a path leading deep into the dark forest from which you emerged. I imagine it was a difficult thing once upon a time to find your people fairly, even with a map. But times have changed. Development means so many of these trees are gone. And drones make it so, so easy to map the rest, to plot a course.

I'll compare this map with satellite imagery and—enhance, enhance, enhance—your old guardians of the deep, dark woods become nothing more than the villain-of-the-week on some crime procedural. Cue screaming guitar riff and roll credits over gnarled branches and knots on trees resembling faces.

As with your secrets, finding this treasure of wealth, power, and wonder beyond human comprehension—if I'm reading these runes correctly—will seem basic in retrospect. Once you know where to check, it's as good as done.

One last thing. I need to get rid of this black smudge here and—

Dammit. Damn you.

Not a smudge at all, right? More bees.

Were they always there? The whole time you wore this face, did you keep these bastard bees under your skin?

When we got placed on the same trivia team at the bar because both sets of friends we'd expected to show bailed on us, were they inside you? When you hid under the red woolen blanket while we watched creepy, old horror movies on the couch and you told me you wanted to show me something, and I knew it was a telegraphed excuse for a kiss, what'd the bees sound like then?

Could they feel my tongue pressing against wet skin, moving past your teeth, manipulating the insides of your cheeks? Every pockmark indentation I touched within your mouth, was it you biting the skin in anticipation of what we'd do? Or was it the bees, trapped in the space between, trying to get out? Or trying to keep the treasure map safe, hidden away from mortal eyes?

I suppose it makes sense. Your people and bees working together. Matriarchal societies both, from what I understand. I've stayed up late considering this and I have a whole theory, but we don't have time.

It's late. And moving toward dawn. Moving to the time when the moon fades under the stunning brilliance of the sun. And my window will close.

I can't wait another day. I want to visit where you've come from and take what I'm entitled to. Because I never signed any paper saying I *couldn't* take what was mine. What I'm entitled to from what was ours.

"We'll be together forever after all," we'd said in unison, smiling with imperfect teeth. It's hard to say which of us was lying.

Maybe it was both of us.

Hospital bills, no job, not sure what to do next. There's the mantra I want hanging over my kitchen instead of 'Live, laugh, love'. Because it's all I've known since you went away, slunk back to a mother and father who were never even yours.

And why did you even leave me in the first place?

Was your real family responsible? Did they lead you away from me? From us? If there's no treasure, no sparkling, impossible diamonds, then I'll settle for revenge. I'll settle for telling them all I hope they choked on the babe they took in your stead, or they broke out in hives at its touch. One way or another, I want them to suffer for letting you go.

Surprised? Don't try to hide it. I know every expression you wear from outside and in. You're not sure why I'd defend you against your people, right? You shouldn't need to wonder.

I love you.

But I want what's meant for me. You were created to

sow discord, to leave sorrow in your wake. And you have. Oh God, you have. But I am no yeoman farmer on the edge of the woodlands, no villager sleeping with one eye open for fear of my goddamn superstitions. I'll take from your people, as they've taken from me. And I'll do it by whatever means necessary. The crimson-stained knife on the Formica kitchen countertop here should remind you how serious I can be.

So, now it's time to get up. Come on. I know you're fine, remember? I know this face was never yours. I know it's now less a face and more a map. It'll guide me to your people, your treasures, and I'll get what I deserve. All my gear's packed in the rucksack over there. Grabbed a few things for you too.

I'm gonna take another look at the map before I go. Just— Ouch.

Ow.

They stung me. Tiny, fuzzy, buzzing bastards. Look at 'em now. Dead at my feet. Hope it was worth it.

What do you think?

What do you...?

Oh. I see.

Those were more than ordinary bees, huh?

What's in those stingers then?

Come on, tell me. Tell me while I take a minute and sit beside you here in the corner. Let me put my head on your shoulder. Turn and face me.

One more kiss?

No?

Here's your face, then. Your old, stolen face. Take it. Go on, take it. You're standing after all. You must be strong enough to take back this face.

What do you mean, you don't want it anymore?

Where are you taking me with all this honey, all those bees, and this face? Isn't this your face?

This isn't my face.

Don't make me wear it. It's covered with bees.

I'll keep your secrets. I swear.

Look at my face and find truth carved deep inside. Follow the lines from my brow to the dimples of my cheeks, to the scar on my chin where I fell in the woods. Not your woods, but some other woods from my childhood. A jagged splinter from a tree stump disappeared inside me and they never got it out. Maybe that's what brought you to me. I carry a piece of your world inside.

My features already form a map, one visible for all the worlds to see. It's led me to this moment with you.

I don't need to wear another.

MAGGOTY WOOD

By Teagan Olivia Sturmer

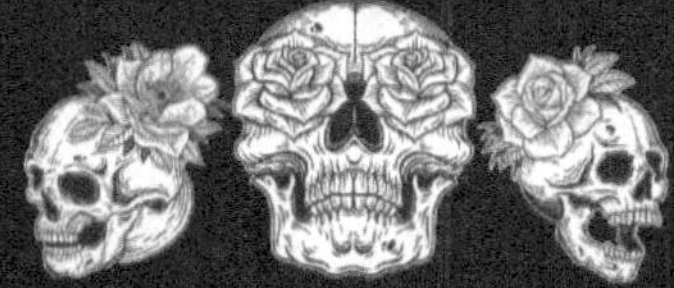

Catherine Wallace has never believed in gods. Never felt the need to bend a knee to the dirt and whisper words she was sure would never be listened to. But here, in the woods, between the hawthorn and silver beeches, she wonders if maybe gods are real.

Or, at least, if devils are.

A wind howls down through the branches overhead and her fingers tighten around the hand she's holding.

"Chill, Cait. Damn, it's like you've never been in the woods before." Her fiancé, Will, leads her through the maze of decaying undergrowth, his leather Oxfords cracking on dropped limbs, the leaves like withered tombstones.

She wrinkles her nose at the back of his head. Of course she's been in the woods before; she just hasn't been in woods like these. Blackened husks of old trunks twist up to meet the leafy canopy like curls of smoke. But the leaves are not green. Not as they should be in the heat of August. They curl gray and sickly, and the grass at Cait's feet seems to crumble with each step she takes. Crows nest in the high branches, their feathers mangy and molting silver in the thin streams of sunlight breaking through to brush the ground below.

But it isn't just these things making Cait's stomach swim and her head reel. It's the sense that something is pressing on her shoulders, perched there like a thing with wings, and she doesn't know when it will wrap hands around her throat and choke her, but she's sure it will.

"How much farther to your parents' house?" she asks, the words half-caught in her throat.

Will stops, spins around. There's a strange gleam in his eye. Something Cait has never seen before. She knows this trip is stressful for Will. She's been asking to meet his parents ever since he got down on one knee, and he's been giving her the same answer since. No.

No, I'm sure they're busy.

No, I can't get away from work that weekend.

No, they're not like your parents, Cait. They're not normal.

No, no, no, no, no.

But she pushed and pried and finally found a phone number tucked between old band t-shirts and work slacks and called it. It was a land line, crackly and fragile when it finally connected.

Yes, yes, Mr. and Mrs. Crane would love to meet her. It must have just slipped William's mind to tell them of the engagement. Wouldn't they love to come visit? Sometime in August perhaps, maybe even for Lammas celebrations?

Cait wasn't sure what Lammas was, but she scratched the dates along a white sheet of paper and when Will found out, he was furious. But after a week, he relented, only made her promise one thing and one thing only.

That she wouldn't eat or drink anything without his approval.

"Oh, so you're expecting your parents to murder me by poison," she teased.

And the look he gave her made her wonder if her joke wasn't so far from the truth.

Will's fingers tighten, white-knuckled, around hers now

and she wants to pull away—he's hurting her—but she stays, stares at his wide, wild eyes.

"Will, did you hear me—?"

He flinches as a crow calls from the branches of an oak, then turns back to the path—if it can even be called a path—dragging her behind him.

"It's only a little farther," he says, and points to a crude sign carved from a stone, painted in white, dripping letters.

MAGGOTY WOOD.

Cait hadn't found it on any map.

It's nearing dark when they reach the edges of the village. Sweat drips down between Cait's shoulder blades, pooling at the waist of her jeans. A dark circle clings to the back of Will's gray t-shirt and she can see stains bleeding out from beneath his arms. The woods are different here, carved back to allow for a ring of houses—maybe twelve at most—built from rock and reed thatching. Each door is painted the exact same shade of blood red. They glisten, almost wetly, in the evening sun. Cait swallows, throat jagged. She leans in to brush lips against Will's ear.

"Are you sure this is your parent's village?" she asks.

He does not answer, but his fingers crush hers, and before she can pull away the doors to the houses break open and they are greeted by dozens of faces. Some young, some old, but all stained with hunger; thin, gaunt, the hollows of their eyes bruised violet.

The breath catches in Cait's throat.

A woman wearing a tattered, blue apron embroidered with little yellow flowers picks a barefoot baby up to her hip and shrinks back into the darkness behind the door. Cait smells woodsmoke and burnt herbs, and something that reminds her of wet, upturned soil. She fights the quick breath seizing in her chest.

"Is this—? Are your parents part of a cult?" she whispers.

Will plasters a saccharine smile on his face and turns back to her. "I told you they weren't normal."

Cait runs through a hundred things that could be viewed as not normal but are also not a fucking cult, and is interrupted by a cry.

"William!"

Cait's eyes snag on a thin woman with salt-and-pepper hair dressed in white and sage green running toward them, arms outstretched. She throws her spindly limbs around Will's neck, pulling him in. He drops Cait's hand, and she stands there, stupidly, alone. No one else approaches them; no one else leaves the safety of their bloodred doors.

"And this must be Catherine," the woman says, leaving the embrace of her son to fling her arms around Cait.

Cait stumbles, feels the strength of the woman's grip, smells the rosemary in her hair.

"Cait," she manages. "It's just... It's Cait."

The woman pulls away, wrinkles her eyes. She studies Cait's face, something sparking in the darkness of her pupils that Cait does not recognize. Something akin to hunger. "Oh, my darling, you are not *just* anything." She smiles, takes Cait's hand. "Call me Eve."

Eve.

The name tastes foreign on Cait's tongue. She stares at Eve, the curl of her pale lips, the freckles dusting the bridge of her nose, the strange scars that dot a line across her forehead like some fleshy crown. The older woman seems to catch her gaze and the ghost of a smile whispers across her lips. She winks.

"Where's Dad?" Will asks.

If the circle of houses wasn't quiet before, it goes silent as a grave at his words. A few of the red doors slam shut, and Cait feels something twist in her belly. Eve turns to look at her son, any gleam now sapped from her eyes.

She doesn't answer for a long time, and Cait can see that a heavy weight rests on the older woman's shoulders.

Will's face twists. "No..." he whispers, the sound long and strained.

Eve reaches a finger up to the trace the line of scars on her skin.

"He's gone to the wood," she says, and kisses her finger.

Cait waits for an explanation, waits for Will to ask when his father is getting back, waits on herself to ask, *aren't we already in the wood?* But no one says anything. Will just angles his head to look further past the circle of homes to the line of ailing, withered trees, his cheeks already stained with tears.

Cait doesn't know what to do. Helplessness breeds in her belly.

Silence rings through the grove. No birds here, hardly any green and growing things, just tangles of dead matter. Of vines that look crisp with winter's bite.

Eve claps her hands together, Cait's heart stabbing a short tattoo against her ribs. "Why don't we get your things inside and then see what we can't come up with for you two for dinner? Everyone is just so excited that you're here." She reaches for Cait's pack, but Cait only holds it that much tighter. "Especially you, my darling."

Cait's skin shudders as Eve leads them to one of the red doors. Will follows his mother inside, but Cait... Cait stays on the step for a moment, eyes trailing the rest of the houses, the well in the center, the dark shadows dancing at the tree line.

There's nothing to worry about, she tells herself. *You're only here for three days. You can do anything for three days.*

She goes to follow Will into the house, but something snags on the edge of her vision. A flash of color—many colors— muted and drifting like paint through smoke. They hover at the tree line as if to say, *watch out, you should have turned back long ago*. And then they're gone, vanishing as a beam of sun breaks through the crumbling canopy. A crow calls from somewhere deep in the forest and Cait feels a prick at the nape of her neck. She tightens her hands around her pack.

Maggoty Wood, indeed.

No one should name the trees.

Inside, the house smells of earth. Haze licks along the low rafters, collecting in pockets and filling each room with the scents of rosemary, sage, and thyme. An orange cat hisses and squeezes itself beneath an overstuffed ottoman.

"Ignore Igraine," Eve says, waving her hands wistfully at the pluming smoke. "She's not used to other bodies."

Cait reaches for Will's hand, but he's already pressing deeper into the bowels of the house.

"Come on," he says. "I'll show you my old room."

Cait's feet slap against the wooden floorboards as she peels away a sock and winces at the blisters turning purple on her heel. The bed sways as she lowers herself onto it, sighing at the coolness of the sheets beneath her skin. Faded flowers are painted on the whitewashed ceiling—yellow daisies, pink roses, blue lupines.

"Did you paint those?" she asks, trying to lighten the mood as Will huffs a sigh and throws his bag onto a wooden rocker.

"What?" His voice is irritated, sharp. He sighs again and lays down beside her on the bed. "Sorry, I'm... No, I didn't. Mum did, I think, when I was a baby. She wanted a girl."

Cait rolls onto her elbows. "So, when were you going to tell me your parents are part of a cult?"

As soon as she says it, she knows it's a mistake. Will's face pains; he shifts a hand beneath his head, remnants of grief still in his eyes.

"I'd hoped it would never come up."

Cait drops back down to the bed, eyes trained once more on the ceiling. She shouldn't have done this. Shouldn't have forced her way into things between Will and his parents. Shouldn't have gone snooping and made that phone call. Shouldn't have made Will buy those train tickets and take that taxi and make the hike through the damned woods to this... This *place*.

"I'm sorry," she says finally, the words heavy like weights on her tongue.

Will blows air from between his lips. "It's fine. You were gonna find out anyway. Let's just get through the next few days as best we can, and Cait?" He grabs her hand, reaches up and curls fingers around her jaw so that she's looking at him. "Remember, don't eat or drink anything without letting me know. Please."

She wants to think it's just a joke. But there's something glimmering in Will's eyes, something wet and pleading, and she realizes it's tears. She squeezes his hand, lifts it to her lips and plants a kiss in the center of his palm.

"I promise."

Sun bleeds light into the center of the houses. They are old; Cait can see that now. Some wilt to the side like forgotten plants. Others collect moss and lichen between their stones like unkempt teeth. And the red doors—she realizes—the red doors are tongues. She's been sitting on the front stoop to Eve's cottage long enough to know the sound of them licking open, shut, open, shut, as people go about their business.

No one looks at her. In fact, they try everything in their power *not* to look at her, making it so obvious she'd rather they did. She wants to say hello, wants to smile as a line of young girls trail by in smocks of white and lemon yellow, bodies so emaciated they look like barren trees. But she doesn't. She just sits there, half-listening to Will and his mother taking tea at the small wooden table in the garden.

It isn't so much a garden as it is a tangle of plants. There are herbs—Cait can smell them—and then there are flowers. Or the remnants of flowers. Husks of seed pods cling to graying stalks. The stem of a hollyhock shakes brittle in the wind, cracking and snapping as it's beaten nearer to the earth.

But it's the smell that Cait focuses on. Something akin to mold. A thick, dusty smell.

She wonders what it is, what's causing it. It seems to simmer up from the ground, as if the sun is baking it right out of the dirt. Except the sunlight is weak beneath the trees and Cait has a feeling that even in the wintertime the village smells like death.

Cait leans back against the stoop, elbows digging into the grit of the hewn rock. She studies the shadows dancing between the trees, the way moss clings to the trunks, making them appear bulbous and swollen like plague limbs.

She wonders...

"How did this place get its name?" she asks, angling toward the garden.

Eve smiles, a slow, practiced thing. She raises a finger, pointing somewhere beyond them. "It's the ground," she says. "It gets sick when we don't feed it."

Cait follows the gesture and something cold needles between her ribs. The trees stand like ghouls, taunting fear at the corner of one's eye. Cait wants to look away, but she can't.

She can't explain it, but she's sure the smell—the dead smell—is coming from the trees, seeping up from the soil beneath them.

"Their god," Will huffs the words. He gestures near his feet. "The ground."

God. The word is like oil and vinegar on Cait's tongue. She catches it between her teeth, trying to swallow it down, but it tastes sour, clogs her throat.

Eve tuts, plinks a meager cube of sugar into her weak tea and swirls it around and around. "You say that as if you no longer believe, William."

"I don't."

Eve takes a long drink, dragging the liquid between her lips and across her tongue, down her throat. "You will again, I'm sure of it." She winks over at Cait. "Don't you worry."

But Cait *is* worried, that's exactly what she is, because it's thicker now—the dead smell—and it seems to be coming right for her.

That night, after a simple dinner of potatoes and herbs, Will argues with Eve. Cait sits on the bed, studying the flower patterns on the ceiling, wondering if she stood on the mattress and stretched up onto her tiptoes the paint would smell like soil, like the dead scent buried beneath the trees.

"I'm not taking her," Will says.

Cait can tell he's trying to whisper, trying to keep his voice low so that she cannot hear, but he's doing a terrible job.

"She is already here, William," Eve is saying, her voice as cool and soothing as mint. "It has been willed."

There is silence. Cait idly chews on the nails of one hand, imagining Will tapping his fingers on the grain of the table, gnawing on his bottom lip.

We shouldn't have come, we shouldn't have come, we shouldn't have come, she repeats to herself, needling her fingernails through the lines on her palms.

She's about to get up, to grab their bags where they still sit packed on the wooden rocker, and tell Will they can march back through the woods in the dark for all she cares, they're going home, when she hears him speak. His voice is so low it might taste of roots.

"It is dead. Your rituals aren't doing anything. Ground is just ground, and it's so overworked out here it's turned to dust. Just because Dad was stupid enough to drag a knife across his own throat and call it a 'sacrifice', doesn't mean I'm willing to do the same. And Cait is an outsider." He pauses. "She has no idea what she's walked into."

Cait's breath hitches in her chest, cold fingers closing around her throat. She wets her lips with the tip of her tongue, tries to piece together the insanity that just spilled from Will's mouth. Sacrifice? A knife across his own throat?

Her breathing returns, scattered like dust on the wind. She tries to calm her racing heart, digs fingernails into the soft flesh of her thigh until they form a circle, unbroken. Eve's voice breaks through.

"Your father did what he knew was best. What was *needed*. Our crops are failing, William. The animals are dying. We almost starved last winter. We will if she—"

Her voice is tired, pleading, and it drips across Cait's arms like garden slugs. She shudders, tries to wipe them off.

"Do you know...?" Will starts, his voice hot, sharp, like freshly forged steel. "If you walk six miles that way there's a village with a shop and you wouldn't have to believe in your dirt god to help your fucking corn grow?"

"William—"

"No, you know what—"

Cait flinches as something slams against the kitchen table and then chair legs screech across wooden floorboards. Will's footfalls are heavy as they come toward her, echoing against the low ceiling. A doomed tattoo.

He appears in the doorway, all his edges shadowed in the dim light that streams in behind him. Cait bites back a moan, feels it gather like jagged rock in the back of her throat. His jaw punches out from beneath his skin, eyes fixed hard on her, then over to the bags.

"We're leaving," he says.

He picks up his pack and tosses the other at her. She flinches again, her skin still swimming with the slugs of Eve's voice. She wraps her hand around the handle of her pack.

"I'm sorry. I shouldn't have—"

"Doesn't fucking matter," Will says, his voice edged and gruff. "We're leaving. Now."

He slings his bag around his shoulders, and she follows suit, shuffling behind him as he heads back toward the kitchen.

But something is wrong.

Eve is not there.

She should be sitting at the kitchen table drinking her meager tea plucked dead from her tangled garden. She should be teary-eyed, begging them not to leave, begging them to stay, saying she's sorry, she'll love Will no matter what he believes. But she's not and the house is empty. Not even a glimpse of orange hair, of feline eyes glinting in the dark.

A China teacup spills milky liquid across the table and the tallow fat candle flickers in a gust of wind that licks in from the open door. Cait's fingers reach for Will's, shaking, her chest now filled with stabbing pain.

Something is very wrong.

Will makes small steps toward the door, his arm outstretched, wrapped around her middle. Her mouth is dry, like sandpaper, and then the air fills with something.

The sound of drums. The scent of smoke.

"Shit." Will holds her back, away from the door, but she stands on her tiptoes, eyes straining over the top of his shoulder.

A mob of bodies gathers in the glade of houses, some clutching the wooden hands of brush torches. Their faces undulate in the flame, shadows dancing, mounting, twirling like living things. Their faces are hollow, but they look at her with hope. With hunger.

A figure stands separate, out in front, bathed in orange light. Cait would think it a woman, if not for the deer skull that rests atop its alabaster shoulders, antlers like a crown piercing flesh, the black-hollow eyes trained on Cait.

"Will..." The name comes out twisted, thin as smoke. Cait tries to heave a breath but only becomes more tangled in the fear that rolls off her body like steam. "Will, what's going on?"

But he doesn't answer. He can't and when she looks up, she's sees why. His eyes are bulging, blood shot through white. His lips gape open and shut like a fish. Open, shut, open, shut. And there is something around his neck, something dark and thick like rope. But it isn't rope. She knows by the way it smells like wet soil and worms that it is a root.

She drops her bag, screeching, scrabbling at Will's throat with her fingers, but the root won't budge. Sweat breaks out at the base of her neck, beads down her spine. Her breathing turns ragged, stunted, like a sawn-off limb. A clear line of spittle glistens from the corner of his lips and she opens her mouth to scream, but no sound emerges, just another rush of hot breath.

"Catherine Wallace."

The name thrums through the glade like a broken harp string. Cait freezes, too scared to take her eyes from Will's choked throat. But then the voice calls to her again—softer this time, reminding her of raw honey scraped from the comb, of spring rain on blooming roses, of upturned soil ready for planting—and she turns.

The figure in the skull mask is closer now, mere inches from her. Breath steams from between the dark hollows and the faint scent of blood mixed with something floral floats along on the wind. Cait swallows, feels the lump in her throat melt as she stares into the black voids of the skull's eyes.

"Catherine," it says again, and the sound is like light rain, like streams of sunlight, like green sprouting from dirt.

Cait drops her hands from Will's throat, and she hears him struggling to say something, struggling to stop her, but there are roots around his wrist now, holding him to the house. Cait drifts forward and the figure holds out a hand—a human hand—and lifts a chalice.

"Drink," the figure commands. "Drink for our vitality. For our healing. Drink so that you may feed."

Cait knows she shouldn't, hears Will's voice somewhere in her mind. *Don't eat or drink anything without letting me know.* She turns to look at him and he says nothing, the root now a gag between his lips.

He knows, she thinks. *He knows it is safe to drink, otherwise he would stop me.*

The figure crooks a finger, offers the cup.

Cait is suddenly so thirsty. She cannot remember when she last ate or drank. Water at the roadside? Tea on the train? Her stomach grumbles, her tongue stretched like desert in her mouth. She reaches for the cup, her movements like honey in the herbed smoke that roils from the torches. Will groans behind her, struggles against his earthen bounds.

She turns to him, her body slow, viscous. She smiles, a cracked thing, like the white of an eggshell.

"Don't worry," she soothes. "You know."

His eyes bulge, wild, but it's too late. She's already taking the cup to her lips. The liquid teases wet, warm, almost reminding her of blood. But it is sweet. So sweet. She opens her mouth, lets the stuff pour in over her tongue, coating her teeth, dripping down the back of her throat to slosh down to her belly.

It tastes of flowers, of muddled lupine and sweet roses and the crisp scent of daylilies. She drinks until the cup is empty, until the liquid runs dark down her chin. She pulls the chalice away, lets it fall from her fingers, stumbles in the light from the torches.

The glade turns hazy, colors mixing like paint. She turns to the line of trees. They reach to her, their limbs like ribcages. The world spins and she laughs.

"Hello, old wood," she whispers. "I can feed you."

The figure in the deer skull slips the chalice into the folds of their robe and holds out a hand.

"It is waiting for you," the figure says, and for a moment Cait recognizes the voice like some remnant of a lost thought.

Call me Eve, the voice had once said. And Cait had. But that was all a fever dream. This, this is reality. She is awake for the first time in her whole life.

She lets the figure wrap cold fingers around hers and lead her to the line of trees. They shudder with each step she takes. When they reach the trunks, the figure turns them back to face the crowd and Cait sees a man amongst them, a man with a root between his teeth. Her eyes moisten and though she doesn't know why, the sight of him makes her body ache.

A fever dream, she reminds herself.

"Long ago, our ancestors found this place, discovered the magic that wound itself between the roots at our feet. It brought us health and prosperity. Food for our bellies, shelter for our bodies, salvation for our souls." The figure holds out a hand. "We only had to do one thing in return. Feed it. Keep it from getting too hungry. For if it did, it would consume everything above, and we would be left with nothing."

Wind rustles the dead leaves and Cait looks up, sees the very air itself dancing with energy now. Energy that wants her. Needs her.

"But as the earth has grown old, it has also grown hungrier. It waits beneath our feet, waits for us to feed it, and when once one body was enough to keep it sated, two are now called."

Silence follows the voice, other than the moaning of the man with the root in his teeth. Cait wonders at him, but the heat from the torches blazes in her eyes and she looks away, back toward the trees. Something flickers there in the darkness. Her skin sparks.

"We have long awaited someone who could feed the dirt. My husband—" Her voice cracks. "My husband was not enough. And so, we will offer up another."

A hand comes to kiss Cait's cheek, soft and light as downy feathers. She looks up and it's human eyes she sees now, human eyes beneath a crown of antlers piercing into flesh beneath the skull mask.

"Catherine Wallace, are you ready?"

Cait has never been ready for a thing in her life. She has always done things without asking, forgiveness easier to seek than permission. She smiles and nods, and the man with the root in his teeth screams as best he can.

The figure in the skull mask lets go of Cait's hand and bends low to scrape nails across barren earth.

"She is coming to join you," the figure says. "Send forth your messenger so that he may take her down to the ground."

For a moment, nothing happens. Wind stirs in the trees, a cold, dusty scent swirling around Cait's throat. Then the ground cracks open like a mouth and spits out a dead man.

Or rather, he *should* be dead.

He doesn't move at first, wrapped in a mottled cloak of reds and yellows. The wind burrows harder, that scent of decay Cait smelled earlier now trailing up her feet, her legs, her spine, to slip into her nose and fill her lungs.

With the snapping of bone, the dead man stands. He is wobbly at first, like a freshly birthed calf covered in mother's viscera. He steps forward, one lazy eye trained on Cait. And she should be terrified. She should run into the trees shrieking and never turn back. But something holds her to the ground. Her stomach rumbles.

She is hungry too.

The dead man approaches, leans forward, a ruin of

mangled bones and maggot-pocked skin, and for a moment Cait thinks she sees something reminiscent of the man with the root between his teeth in what little features he has left. He smiles—or tries to—dirt breaking free from his blackened gums and crumbling down over his exposed ribs.

"Welcome, newest daughter," he says, in a voice that seems to come up from the ground itself. "Welcome to the Maggoty Wood."

Behind her, somewhere, she hears a scream. It is a funny thing. She thinks it sounds familiar. She turns and sees the man on his knees, a root wrapped around his middle now, around his arms, pulling him to the ground. He has tears in his eyes. She can see them glistening in the fireglow, and she feels a sort of sadness spread itself in her belly like a burial shroud. She knows him, or at least, a part of her did. A part of her that wasn't made of roots and soil.

A fever dream.

She can feel it crawling up her shins now, turning her blood to mere remnants of dirt.

To dust, she thinks.

The rotting man lifts a palm, presses bony fingers streaked with black to her forehead.

"So that we may grow," he says, his voice slippery with earth worms.

"So that we may grow," the people in the glade respond.

And Cait feels the ground take her to her knees, feels the earth snap at her skin. She is not afraid, even though the man behind her is screaming her name over and over and over. But is it really her name? Does it even ring true in her ears anymore as she hears it?

Cait, Cait, Cait, she hears, and it sounds funny, like the shattering of glass.

The earth rips up through her stomach, her chest, breaking out through her mouth as a root flicks the surface of her lips and breaks out into the night.

No, she is not Cait. Not anymore. She is of the wood now. Of the earth.

"Welcome," the dead man says, his breath now smelling of iron, of blood. "Taste the ground."

And she does. The root rips her mouth, her cheeks, shredding flesh from bone until her teeth lay exposed, and she smiles. Smiles as she collapses into the dirt, feels the worms and maggots glide nearer on hungry bellies. Feels the trees reach out to her with aching limbs.

You will feed us, they say. *You will make us grow strong so we can keep our people safe.*

And she will.

She will feed the wood.

OLD MAN VREEN

By TJ Price

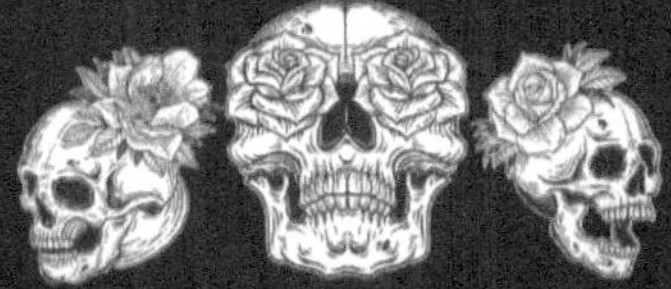

In order to get to the lot, one had to drive a good distance out of Bracken into the unnamed Township 59, through endless grasping wilderness, until the dirt drive became impassable to most vehicles.

This was where Colson had been contracted—the depths of the woods, where not even a fool would want to build a house.

Yet some fool had decided this very spot would be the location to put down roots, and some other fool had decided to assist the first fool by leveling and razing a patch of the leafy forest for them to transport their materials.

World's full of fools, Colson thought.

He hefted the chainsaw again and fought to hold it in place as it gutted into the old beech tree. The trunk was at least as big around as a man was tall, and a strange twinge of shame wormed at him as he sawed at its belly. Dust and shavings spat up around him. They landed on the kerchief over his mouth and flew past his safety glasses.

He'd felled hundreds of trees before. Why was this one any different?

Why, for that matter, were any of them in this forest?

Krrrrrrr-ACK!

Even after Colson saw that the tree had hit the ground, the sound of its felling echoed in his skull like a reprimand, and the leaves in the boughs quivered even after the tree's carcass had settled.

There was something weird about these woods. Every man on the team knew it. Even Loudmouth Pete Sevigny was sullenly silent, as if cowed into submission by something unseen. None of the men talked to each other, not even when they all took their union break, around one in the afternoon. They just sat there, silently, chewing their sandwiches, gurgling from their Thermoses.

"Well, if nobody else is gonna say it," Pete finally broke out, toward the end of the break, "it's like fellin' trees in a fuckin' funeral home around here. Jesus Christ." He inserted a toothpick between his teeth and set his face around it in a glower.

The rest of the team nodded or mumbled assent. Ollie Brandt, the youngest of the crew, reached up behind his head and scratched at his neck, avoiding eye contact with Colson, then hesitantly said, "I heard some things about this place, last night at the bar in town."

"The bar in town?" Loudmouth Pete glanced at Ollie. "You're stayin here?"

Ollie looked at Pete, then away. "Yeah, well, my truck wouldn't start last night, so I—"

"You said you didn't need any help," interrupted Reggie, sitting to Ollie's right. "You said it just needed a minute."

"It did," said Ollie hotly, his face pinking, "but it only got as far as town, then it quit on me again, so I just said 'fuck it' and went an' had a drink at the bar. Figured I'd just pass out in my truck. Started up fine this mornin.'"

There was a long pause among the men as they digested the information. Colson stood up, intending to get back to work. Trees wouldn't fell themselves.

"So, you heard some things?" Pete, of course.

"Oh, yeah. So, uh…" Ollie stammered, "these here woods, they're…"

"Get on with it," said Pete, motioning with his hand for Ollie to continue. "Ain't got all day, man."

"Okay, well, the guy told me these woods is haunted by a witch."

Murmuring boiled up among the team.

"A witch?" Pete stared at Ollie with naked hostility. "Quit fuckin' with us, Ollie."

"No," Ollie retorted, with as much vehemence as he could muster. "I ain't. Only, it ain't like, a woman witch. It's a man. Name's Old Man Vreen." He looked at Colson for help, silently pleading.

"Think that's called a 'warlock,' Ollie," said Colson, trying to keep the tired out of his voice. It'd been a long night, and a longer day. A long week.

We've changed. Her voice as clear and sharp as if she were saying it directly into his ear rather than being a memory of days prior. *We just don't want the same thing anymore.*

Colson shook his head to rid himself of the pain, then dug deep into his pocket for his bottle of Excedrin. He tipped out a pill and popped it into his mouth, chewing it down to a chalky paste and swallowing it all at once.

"The guy said he was a witch, so…I dunno," Ollie said, stubbornly. "But he said Old Man Vreen haunts this forest. And he said that we were all in a whole lot of danger bein' out here, cuttin' down the trees like we're doin'."

Ollie paused, looking at Colson again, searchingly.

"C'mon, now," Colson said. "Ain't no such things as witches and warlocks, and there's no such things as haunted woods."

"Old Man Vreen." Reggie spoke up. He lived closest out

of everyone to the site. "Y'know, I remember hearin' somethin' about an Old Man Vreen once, when I was a kid. The town hanged him. Somethin' about the parson's son going missing?"

"'Just a rope, and a man at the end of it,'" quoted Marc Thibodeaux, out of nowhere, in his heavy Quebecois accent. "Yes, I remember this as well. They say the river ran black, and the fields did not make their crops, after the man was hanged."

"Like one of them plagues outta the Bible," Reggie said, without looking at Colson.

"Break's over, fellas," Colson said, and the team started packing up their lunches and pulling their gloves back on, again lapsing into quiet.

But now it was a different kind of quiet, Colson thought.

The shadows of the old beech trees loomed, lengthened.

Once Colson got off the dirt track and back on asphalt, he pulled into the little parking lot in front of the only bar in Bracken. It didn't appear to have a name, only a red neon in the window that advertised the sale of Pabst Blue Ribbon. He unclipped his cell phone from its holster and navigated to search. He typed in 'Old Man Vreen' and hit enter, then waited for the page to refresh.

Something large and wet thwacked into the windshield, right at eye-level, and Colson started, his attention torn from his phone. It was a glob of bird shit. He hit the wipers and watched as they scrubbed the droppings away, leaving only a ghost of the white and gray mess around the edges.

He glanced back down at the phone, which had vibrated in his hand. Instead of the results for his search, there was a text message from EMILY.

I'm sorry.

Colson's vision blurred with sudden tears, and he fought the rising panic in his throat as he read on.

I'll be back soon. Maybe we can talk again when you get back?

This is so hard. I love you.

Colson grit his teeth and fought the urge to smash the phone against the dashboard. His knuckles whitened around the edges. Inhale. Exhale. Inhale. Exhale.

Slowly, gratingly, he centered himself, back to his neutral state. Inhale. Exhale. Innnnnnn…and ouuuuut.

His tensed muscles relaxed, and he started typing a message back when he noticed that his phone said: NO SERVICE.

Of course.

"Goddamnit!" Colson whacked the steering wheel with the knife edge of his hand. Pain seared up and into his shoulder, which was already aching with the weight of the chainsaw he'd been wielding all day.

He needed a drink.

Maybe the bar had Wi-Fi. He choked back a laugh and got out of the truck, slamming the door shut behind him.

Inside was quiet. There was only one other person sitting at the bar. There was a small row of booths, each unoccupied, and a back hallway that looked like it led to the bathrooms. Colson took a seat at the bar, a few away from the other man, and nodded to the bartender.

"Bourbon. Whatever you got in the well's fine, just throw some ice in it, will you?" Colson paused. "Fuck it. Make it a double."

The bartender nodded and pulled out the bottle of Old Crow from the well, then filled a rocks glass with ice and started pouring. "Long day?"

"Long everything," said Colson, putting a point on it. He leaned to one side to fish out his wallet. "What do I owe ya?"

"You're one of those guys working up in the woods, yeah?"

"Uh-huh." Colson stared at the man, his wallet open.

"On the house," the bartender said, waving his hands. "You guys got more trouble than you can handle."

"Uh...alright," said Colson, never one to turn down a free drink. After a moment, he reached back into his wallet, pulled out a few bills, and tossed them on the bar. "Trouble, you say?"

The bartender crossed his arms over his chest. "Didn't your buddy tell you what we told him?"

"No," said Colson, without missing a step. "What do you mean, 'trouble'?"

The bartender shifted from foot to foot, glanced down the bar at the other man, then finally looked to Colson again. "People go missing, y'see."

"Missing? Like, they go hiking and get lost, or...?" Colson took a drink. The bourbon was vicious—it burned—but it had a surprising sweetness too.

"More like they go up and never come back," the other man at the bar said, lifting his head. "They gets taken."

The bartender looked heavy and sad to Colson. "Mister, I'm not tryin' to... I mean, I know firsthand..." He sighed, frustrated, and started over. "Look. You don't wanna be messin' around in those woods, alright? That's all there is to it."

"Gotta," said Colson, and tilted back the rocks glass until just a rattle of ice was left. "It's my job. And it's my men's job, too, so stop tellin' your damned stories about witches and warlocks, all right? You'll get 'em all riled up, and that'll be the end of our gig."

"So ye know about Old Man Vreen," said the man at the bar. His voice was thick and rusty, like an old key turning in an older lock.

"Know enough," Colson said firmly, putting the glass down on the bar and standing up.

"He ain't gonna like ye chopping down his woods," said

the stranger. His voice wavered halfway between a chortle and a sob.

"Well, he ain't the one that signs my paycheck," Colson said. "Now, I'd appreciate it if you'd stop scarin' my men with townie legends."

"Ain't no legend." The bartender had spoken up. "Old Man Vreen was real as you or me. There's even documents in the town hall."

"Were," corrected the man at the bar. "Most of em got all et up in the fire."

"Right," said the bartender. "But you can look and see for yourself. Was an old man, rotted out with crazy, who went to live out there. Never married, never had no kids, just lived in an old shack by himself in them woods. That's when the kids started goin' missin'."

Colson made to go, but stayed. "Kids?" he said, feeling the question coaxed out of him by the silence.

"Kids. Four of 'em, before little Johnny Taylor, the mayor's son," said the bartender. Skreek-skreek went his rag in the clean pint glass he was polishing.

"Snatched," said the man at the bar, his head drooping low over his beer.

"So, the mayor got together all the men in the whole town, and they went into them woods, and they done dragged Old Man Vreen out by the scruff. Hanged him right out there." The bartender pointed past Colson, toward the door. "Right in front of town hall, on that big oak. No cops, no courts. Just a rope, and Old Man Vreen at the end of it."

Silence fell, vast and brutal. The floorboards creaked under Colson's boots, and he stepped back unconsciously. "Jesus," he breathed, then remembered himself. "Did they find the kids?"

"Nope. Not a one of 'em. And when it was done?" The bartender continued on, mercilessly, as if following a script, and Colson felt an instant of sudden vertigo. "The river ran black. Fallow fields refused to hold seed. And then the parson's son vanished from the schoolyard. Right out from under Miss Mary's eyes."

"Witch or warlock, call it what ye want, but whatever's left of Old Man Vreen on this earth still lives up in them woods," said the man at the bar, chiming in as if cued, "and it don't take well to strangers. Ain't nobody who goes up there comes back. Not even the Staties can find 'em."

"Well, I did, and my men all did today too, so there's proof for you," said Colson, his voice still unsteady.

"Are ye sure, Chief?" The man at the bar lifted his head and turned around, displaying an easy smile. "Did ye count 'em as they drove off your little lot?"

"Yes," lied Colson, thoroughly discomfited. "Every man accounted for."

The man at the bar sucked in air through his teeth and shook his head. "Ye're missin' one and ye don't even know it."

"Listen—" Colson began.

"Alright, alright," interjected the bartender. "You've probably had enough, Lawrence. Leave the man alone. There's only so much ye can pour in closed ears."

Colson opened his mouth to say something in response, but instead turned and walked out of the bar into Bracken's evening air.

As he breathed in, it struck him as odd that there was a salty tang to it, though the nearest ocean was hundreds of miles away.

He got in the truck and turned the key in the ignition. Outside, the sun dipped, and the shadows of the trees surrounding moved with it. Night was steadily falling, and with it Colson's desire to drive all the way through the wilderness back to civilization, where he would have to spend another night alone in the soulless Holiday Inn, with all its anodyne lights and cookie-cutter amenities.

No, maybe it would be best if he just slept in the truck, he thought, and tugged his thick Carhartt coat closer to his body. Wouldn't be so bad.

Ollie'd done it, after all.

Even though the red neon on the bar's window emblazoned itself on the backs of his eyelids, the bourbon soothed him.

Before he knew it, his drifting, disconnected thoughts turned to dreams.

He woke with a start, slamming the door on the images he'd seen with such ferocity that he sat up straight in the driver's seat and nearly hit the horn on the wheel by accident.

Blearily, he wiped at his eyes and fumbled for his phone. The lit screen read 02:04AM. There was one new notification, from Emily.

Colson opened up her text messages, and was flooded with a sudden barrage:

Colson

Colson

Colson

Colson

Colson

As he watched his name appear over and over again, alarm mounted, and he fumbled for the option to call her, but the messages stopped, and he saw the three dots that indicated she was typing.

At the top of the screen, the phone still read: NO SERVICE.

"What the fuck...?" Colson watched as the dots disappeared, then reappeared, until finally, one final text floated into being.

im in the woods

Then the screen went dark, and Colson was alone with his breath, pluming like a quill into the air until it hit the glass of the windshield. He'd steamed up the windows with his body heat alone, Colson noticed, and set to rubbing at the driver's side with the cuff of his jacket. It was too late now to head back to the hotel. By the time he reached it, he'd just have to turn around and head back to the site.

He sighed and got out of the truck, using his phone's flashlight to guide him. Bracken, it seemed, had very little money in the budget for streetlights. Only one of them, in the far distance down the street, flickered its jaundiced glow.

Colson had never felt so profoundly alone. The few buildings on the street were dark-eyed and closed-mouthed. The wind roared in the woods beyond, a deep, rasping howl, as though it were searching through the space between the stars rather than between the trees.

He stopped walking. A primal terror took chilly purchase on the root of his body, and his testicles retreated in instinctual fear. His mouth went dry, and his eyes skittered from point to point in the interminable darkness. He had the sudden urge to ask the darkness, *Who's there?* but as soon as the urge crested, he swallowed it as hard as he could.

You don't ask a question when you don't want an answer.

His phone rang. Not the little trill-vrrrr of a text, but the full-fledged marimba of the default ringtone. It startled Colson into dropping the device, and it clattered on the road at his feet. The flashlight winked out, leaving him in total darkness.

The wind rushed in around him, as if trying to fill the vacuum that the phone's little LED light had left behind. He stooped to retrieve it and heard her voice this time, coming out of the phone's little speaker.

"Colson? Colson is that you? Colson?"

He cradled the phone against his face. "Yeah, it's me. Emily? Emily, what's wrong?"

Static blurred the line, though it sounded like Emily was

breathing heavily, as if she was running, or crying.

"Colson?"

Colson stood stock-still. Didn't dare to breathe. Didn't dare to respond. Something had moved, one darkness detaching from another, somewhere on the road in front of him.

"Col-son," Emily's voice came again, this time pitched to a lilt, a dangerous little sing-song.

"NO!" Colson violently threw the phone away, in the direction of whatever had started approaching. The flashlight came on as he did, stabbing out into the blackness, before it went out again, landing somewhere in the distance.

And yet, he heard it again. Her voice, brittle and taunting.

"I'm in the woods," she whisper-sang, directly into Colson's ear.

He slapped where the mouth of the voice should've been, but there was nothing. He broke, and tore back running to the truck. He fumbled, skidded, even scraped his knee, but as soon as his fingers hit the handle, he wrenched the door wide and threw himself inside, slamming it behind him.

The dashboard lit up with a red figure, neatly bisected in two by their seatbelt, and chimed, chiding him to buckle up.

He woke to the sound of someone tapping on his driver's side window. It was Ollie, peering in as though he couldn't see through the glass, both hands cupped around his eyes.

Colson blinked, rubbed at his eyes, then rolled the window down. "Hey, Ollie."

"Hey, uh, Chief. Did you, uh...spend the night here?"

"Yeah, well, you gave it such a good review that I had to try it out myself." Colson cracked his neck, which had developed a hideous crick from the cramped style in which he'd been sleeping.

Ollie didn't laugh. "Your truck wouldn't start neither?" His voice was hushed, like he was trying to keep it a secret. "I swear, everything about it was fine. I even checked under the hood, the alternator, the... It was all fine! Just wouldn't start. Never had no problems with it before."

"Yeah," said Colson. A thought bubbled up through the morning haze. "Say, Ollie... Everyone made it off-site last night, yeah?"

"Yeah, I think so," said Ollie, scratching his head. "Think you was the last one to leave. Didn't know you was plannin' on stickin around, or I would've stayed with you." He cast a sketched glance in the direction of the road leading up to the site. "Shouldn't stay 'round here alone at night, Chief. Don't like these woods. Not one bit."

"Yeah," Colson said. "Here, lemme..." He motioned for Ollie to move away, then rolled up his window and exited the truck, shutting the door behind him. "Did you find a phone out here, by chance?"

"No, uh-uh," said Ollie. "Did you lose yours?"

"Yeah, I uh...last night. Somewhere around here."

Colson looked around, heading towards the spot he'd hurled it, and Ollie followed. The two men looked for a good couple of minutes before Ollie stood up.

"Sorry, Chief. Dunno what happened to it. You sure you didn't leave it in the truck?"

"Yeah, pretty sure. Damnit. Emily called me last night. Or at least, I think Emily called me last night. I dunno. Maybe it was a dream, or something."

Ollie stared at him with his innocent, round eyes. He dusted his hands off on his thighs. "Maybe what was a dream, Chief?"

Colson opened his mouth to recount the weird encounter

he'd had in the night, but then snapped it shut, remembering Ollie's childlike propensity to glom onto any spooky detail and give it a whole new sort of life.

"Nothing," he said eventually. "C'mon, let's get up to the site before Loudmouth Pete and Co. get here."

Colson grit his teeth and plunged into his work. All around him, the whine and snarl of chainsaws as the team diligently hacked and scraped their way through the wilderness, punctuated from time to time by the cry of "TIM-BER!" and followed by the crashing sough of branches and trunk encountering the earth below.

He was so focused, in fact, on getting the job done, that he skipped his first union break. He would've even worked straight through lunch if it hadn't been for Ollie tapping him on the shoulder and telling him what time it was. Colson blinked, shifted his safety glasses back, and stared up at the sky. The sun was mummified, swathed behind layers of gauzy cloud—the light that leaked through was gray and pallid.

Finally, Colson put down his tools and came around to meet the others. He had no lunch to eat, since he'd stayed in his truck overnight, and his stomach made hideous, wet noises. He gratefully accepted some of Ollie's sandwich and some bitter coffee from his Thermos too. It wasn't until he'd sated his hunger that he looked around and realized:

They were a man short.

Colson blinked and rubbed at his eyes. Maybe he'd just missed him, or maybe he was off taking a piss in the woods. "Marc here today?" he asked, cringing at the gravel in his voice. He coughed, trying to even out the sound.

"Nuh-uh," said Loudmouth Pete, uncharacteristically quiet. "Didn't show up this morning."

"Didn't go home last night, neither," said Reggie, his face drawn. "Loretta called me this morning, asked if we went out drinkin' last night. Told her no, not that I knew of, anyway."

Colson didn't know what to say. He dug into his pocket for his bottle of Excedrin, tapped one out, and began chewing it down to powder. "Not like him to ghost," he said, after a swig of Ollie's coffee.

"Thing is," said Reggie, swallowing something in his throat, "his truck's still here."

"What?" Colson's voice broke, shimmying like a spooked horse, and he fought to keep it under control. "What do you mean, 'his truck's still here'?"

Loudmouth Pete pointed towards the array of parked trucks. "Just what he said. See?"

Colson followed Pete's finger to the lot, and sure enough, there was Marc's old Ram, beaten up and spattered with mud, but unmistakably his, with a big Habs logo in the back window.

"Well, fuck, then...where did he go?" Ollie said, bemusement purpling his tone.

"Fucked if I know," said Reggie.

"You don't think..." Ollie started, but then cut a glance at Colson.

"Well, we have to find him," said Colson, grimly, standing up.

"He could be anywhere," said Reggie, after a minute. "We haven't seen him for twenty-four hours. Hell, he coulda walked back to Canada in that amount of time."

"No," said Colson. Stubbornness rose up in him like a cloud, though he had no idea where it came from. "He can't have gone far. If we split up and fan through the forest around here, we'll find him." He paused, then added, "Maybe he just got drunk and passed out somewhere. You know how he gets."

A murmur passed between the three other men. Shifty

eyes sliding to shifty eyes. "If you say so, Colson."

"I do," he said. His headache was harpooning him right through the middle of his head, and he massaged at his temples.

I'm in the woods, he heard Emily's voice say again, filtering through the haze, and he jerked his head to the side, trying to dislodge it.

He wished he had his phone, service or not. Maybe Marc had sent him a message. Maybe he'd received it, somehow.

Thinking of his phone, lost to the night, made him think of Emily. Maybe he could convince her to come back to him. Maybe they could patch things up, make a real go of it. Maybe he'd even make an honest woman out of her.

But he didn't have his phone. And he didn't have Emily.

Colson shook his head even harder. He needed to focus. One of his men was missing, and it was his duty to find him.

"C'mon," he urged the three remaining. "Let's get going. We don't have time to waste."

The men grumbled, but each of them got up and followed Colson into the woods, one after the other. Even Loudmouth Pete.

"Don't go too far," Colson said. "Just far enough that I can still hear you calling."

Neither Loudmouth Pete nor Reggie made any kind of crack. Their faces were unhappy, but they nodded, and trudged off into the woods on their own paths.

The trees thickened as they went—not in number, but in girth—and the ancient giants dwarfed them. The woods were a minefield of sticklebur too, and Colson could feel them sticking to his clothes as he made his way through.

Every moment or so, Colson would hear the echoes

of the other men, spread out from him, calling out their lost crewmate's name.

"MARC!" An echo of Pete's voice barked like a dog. The sun spun hazy circles overhead.

"MARC!" An echo of Reggie's voice, a bit too far, Colson worried. It sounded slightly faint.

"MARC!" Ollie's voice, from right behind him.

Colson jumped and spun around. "Ollie! Jesus Christ, you scared the fuck out of me."

"Sorry," the younger man cringed. "I just was worried about, y'know, getting lost, so I guess I just started followin' you."

Colson listened for the echoes. Reggie, then Pete. Pete, then Reggie. "We'll cover more ground if you head off on your own."

"MARC!"

"I don't wanna go," said Ollie, fidgeting with something in his hands that looked like a ball and a bunch of twigs at the same time. "I don't wanna get taken, like the others."

Colson kept quiet, thinking about his encounter the night prior. His steps were heavy, and his eyes felt like they were filled with sand. "What's that, Ollie?"

"What's what?" Ollie blinked up at Colson.

"That thing, in your hand. What is that?"

"Oh, I found it on Marc's truck. It's kinda neat. You wanna see?"

Ollie handed the thing to Colson. It was a ball of twigs. Somehow, the small branches had been bent around and woven into one another without breaking. The tension of the thing made Colson feel dizzy, as if it was about to snap apart at any moment. Slowly, he handed it back to Ollie, then paused.

"What's wrong, Chief?" Ollie asked.

"The others," Colson said. "I don't hear the others anymore."

The woods were quiet. The sun went behind a cloud, and Colson felt the chill of its absence creep up his back.

"REGGIE! PETE!" he hollered, hands cupped around his mouth.

But there was no response. Just the silky susurrus of leaves in the beech trees, whispering amongst themselves.

"This is fucking bullshit," Colson muttered, then tried again. "REGGIE! PETE!" His palms were sweating, and his voice rasped as he shouted.

"Maybe they just gave up and went back to the site," Ollie offered, but his voice had a slight stammer, and Colson noticed that his pupils had gone wide as gaping holes in his face.

"Maybe," said Colson, unnerved. "Fuck."

"M-maybe we oughta do the same thing, Chief?" Ollie's voice was searching, his eyes darting from side to side. "It's gettin' late."

"We have to find Emily," Colson muttered. "She's out here, somewhere."

"Emily?" Ollie stopped walking.

"I meant Marc. Marc. We're looking for Marc." Colson continued walking, shambling, almost, through the brush.

"Chief, I think we oughta—"

Colson stopped mid-shamble and turned around.

Ollie was gone. Where he had stood was just a small tree, little more than a sapling, and on one of its limbs dangled the twig-ball, rocking back and forth in the listless breeze.

"Ollie?" Colson asked, and immediately wished he hadn't. There was a peculiar flatness to his voice, as if the woods had stripped it of an echo.

He took one step backwards, then another, cringing at the noise his boots made in the leaves, all the while keeping a level eye on the small tree. He knew he was drawing attention to himself, but to what ear, he had no idea. All he knew was that he needed to get out of the woods, and fast.

The same feeling of an unseen presence, just as had lurked at the end of the dark road last night, came upon him.

A twig snapped somewhere in the forest, and Colson bolted in the opposite direction. All thoughts of Pete, Reggie, and even Ollie fled from his mind as he ran. Branches struck him in the face, clawing at his skin, and burrs leapt from their stickles to try to slow him down, but he fought through it, panic giving him momentum, until he was tripped by the snaking root of a tree, and fell sprawling on his chin. His jaws rattled, his teeth clipped his tongue, and he gasped, scrambling to his feet and—

Ahead of him, a small wooden shack had sprung out of the ground in a small clearing. He hadn't noticed it before, but he didn't question its sudden appearance, and ran towards it with veering steps. Maybe he could hide out until this threat—whatever it was—had passed. The porch received him with creaking shouts underfoot, and the door swung in with an ungodly shriek, but none of it mattered to Colson, just that it was inside.

He slammed the door behind him and leaned heavily against it, panting as his eyes adjusted to the dim interior.

Slowly, his panic began to recede. Inside wasn't much. A dingy, one-room cabin about the size of a closet, and all the wood that made it up appeared to be rotted.

Wouldn't take much to knock this place over, Colson thought, but at least it was shelter from whatever lurked outside for now.

Colson picked his way over the fungus-riddled floorboards. He was looking for anything to defend himself. A gun, ideally. A blade, a shovel, anything, but there was nothing. Not even a bed, or a hearth. Just a small, whittled-together table and chair, all made from the same wood that comprised the entire shack. There weren't even any windows. The only light that entered streamed in through cracks in the nailed-together walls, or where the wood had fallen away over the years. Beyond, on the other side of the room, was a small door.

A closet, maybe, Colson thought, and lifted the wooden latch.

Within was a flat, black darkness, with what looked like stairs carved out of the earth itself, leading down. Colson's heart trip-hammered at the thought of descending, but down felt even safer than in, so he proceeded, one foot after the other, into the cool, dank cellar. He wished he'd never thrown his phone. He wished he smoked cigarettes, so he'd be carrying a lighter.

But he had nothing other than the dim stripes of light falling in from between the floorboards of the shack upstairs, and they illuminated nothing but a large, open space, empty as far as Colson could see. On the edges of the room, roots feathered into the air like exposed nerve endings.

It's like some kind of preparatory chamber, Colson thought.

As though the room was meant for something, some kind of act or ritual, but lay dormant. Waiting to be used.

His throat tightened at the thought, and he turned away from the awful room, revolted by its wrongness. He headed back up the stairs to the shack, but the door had shut behind him, and no amount of jockeying the handle back and forth or pounding on the wood would get the latch to release.

He drew his fist back from the door, grimacing. The meat of it had come into contact with something sticky, something slimy, something that transferred to his fingertip when he touched it.

Then something came out of the corner, a ghastly rush of fetid odor, but all that Colson could see of it was the impression of a face with eyes protruding from its skull and ligature marks imprinted redly around its putrescent, bulging neck...

Colson screamed, but there was no one left to hear him.

"I don't understand it," said Bruce Sevigny, twisting his Rolex on his hairy wrist. "I've never seen anything like it. Why would they just up and leave like this? Where would they even go?"

State Trooper Scanlon shrugged, and stuck his finger in his ear. The blackflies were getting worse. It was that time of the year, when the heat started to crank up. It had taken him hours to drive up to Bracken to investigate the disappearance of the work crew, and he wasn't pleased about having to drive the whole way back by day's end.

"Listen, Bruce," Trooper Scanlon said, his voice as heavy as his footstep, "maybe they all just got drunk and went out into the woods. If they did, my team will find 'em. I've got my partner out there searching for any trace, any clues they might've left behind. Rest assured, we'll find them, all right?"

Bruce looked down his nose at the trooper. He didn't take kindly to being called by his first name, and the trooper could tell through the narrowing of the man's eyes.

"My son was one of them," Bruce said, "so you understand, this is a personal effort. I'd appreciate any manpower you Staties can offer."

"Okay," the trooper said, nonplussed by the man's overt attempts to manipulate him, through infamy or otherwise. "I'll do what I can, but I can't promise nothin'. We're thin on the ground as it is these days, and it takes quite a while to haul up to Bracken, so..." He avoided the man's grayish stare. "I'll see what I can do."

"Yeah, you do that," said Bruce gruffly, and looked down at his hands.

Only a moment of awkward silence squeezed between them when a voice erupted from out of the woods.

"FUCK! DERRICK! GET OVER HERE!"

It came from behind them, past the edge of the woods, past the largest of the felled trees.

"Oh... Oh fuck..."

This was the voice of the trooper's partner, and at the sound of it, both men snapped to attention.

They only had to run a small distance before they came on the scene.

Officer Nealon stood at the base of an enormous beech tree, its smooth trunk extending at least fifty feet above. But it wasn't what was in the treetops that drew Nealon's eye, nor was it what drew Bruce or Trooper Scanlon's. It was what hung in the branches.

There, suspended on the thick-muscled arm of the beech, hung all five of the men from the crew, dead at the neck.

Each of them had wedged into their mouths what looked like a ball of twigs.

THEY'LL FIND YOU AND THEY'LL KILL YOU

By Bitter Karella

No one goes to Cat Hole these days because of the worm outbreak. Folks got it from the cats and it made them go funny, start thinkin' strange. That was some a hundred years ago though. Probably ain't no worms there no more—nothing but plain old cats now, if the cats are even still there—but folks steer clear.

The only church on the mountain is in Cat Hole. They don't use it as a church anymore, of course, and they say the reverend turned his back on the old god and smashed the tabernacle when he got the blood worms and started thinking funny. But the land remembers. It's still consecrated ground. And that means, to the Hawkins clan, it still counts.

If you can get to Cat Hole, you just might be safe.

A distant howl grabs your attention and you miss your footing, sliding down the ravine, grabbing desperately at the slick branches of a passing fir tree as you tumble, finally dropping ass-first into the ditch water creek at the bottom of the slope.

Another howl joins the first, and then another. The Hawkins hounds have found your scent. You can't rest.

You lurch to your feet and a sudden sharp, shooting pain

electrifies your left leg. Shit. The fall really fucked you up.

You're ankle deep in water. The stream can hide your scent if you follow it. It might be your best bet. It might be your *only* bet. You stumble forward, slogging through mud and eddies choked with leaves and pine needles. Your leg is throbbing, but you drag it along.

On the ridge above, you can see the shadows of the Hawkins hounds loping through the fog. They're here. Your only hope is that they don't see you yet. Not that the Hawkins hounds, if you can call them that, actually 'see' anything.

They're loping down the ravine on their crooked legs, snapping and whining. They've been bred to be expert sniffers, bred so thoroughly to that end that you can hardly recognize them as dogs anymore. The first few generations, Pa Hawkins just put out their eyes and docked their ears so that they had to rely on smell, but eventually—after breeding sister to brother and mother to son for years—the new Hawkins hounds are born eyeless and earless, with heads smooth and pointed like a shark's.

The lead hound releases a sick, gargling howl as it drops down into the water behind you with a splash.

There's a cave to your left, a short tunnel under the exposed roots of a dead alder tree on the berm.

Another hound drops into the water. You hear it splash.

You clamber out of the stream and squeeze into the cave, smashing your way through the network of dry, exposed roots. Your breath is rattling loud and dry in your lungs as you wait. Your heart sounds like a jackhammer, so loud that you're sure it will give you away. All you can do is wait.

From your cave, you watch as the Hawkins boys come whooping and hollering down the ravine, hot on the heels of their baying hounds. They pound into the stream and there's a brief confusion. The hounds snort and snuffle and wander in circles as the lead boy—it's not Pa Hawkins, that much you can tell from this distance—shouts abuses at them. Eventually, they figure out what you must have done, and they urge the hounds to push downstream.

You pull back into the cave, accidently sitting your full weight on your bum leg. You bite back a scream.

The Hawkins boys are passing now, all intent on the hounds and the stream. Not a one turns to see the cave, or you, huddled in the shadows. You count about eight Hawkins boys. Is that all of them? You're not sure. They're always making more of them. You wait for their shouts and swears to recede into the distance, and you think it might be safe enough to risk a run.

That's when a final straggler staggers by. Number nine, by your count. The straggler is a young lad, no beard on his chin yet. He's naked, but whether he didn't have time to get dressed in the suddenness of the hunting call, or whether he lost his clothing somehow during the excitement of the chase, you have no idea. His alabaster skin positively glows in the moonlight.

It's not the time to think about it, but you can't help but notice the family resemblance. You didn't think about it when Pa Hawkins first brought Priscilla to your attention, but all the Hawkins spawn must take after their mother, since neither Priscilla nor her brothers bear any resemblance to that big, hairy giant.

The straggler is a dead ringer for Priscilla, actually, other than the dick flopping between his legs, and it's weird how the same pale skin and limp, white hair that look so radiant on Priscilla during the day can look so sinister on her brother in the dark.

The straggler pauses, standing shin-deep in the flow of the creek, sniffling and snorting, as if he can taste you on the air. He turns to stare in your direction, but you know the Hawkins boys have bad eyes. They can barely see in the light; they probably can't see for shit in the dark.

He probably can't see you here.

But then he lunges, arms flailing, mouth gaping, his feet moving so fast that for a moment he almost seems to be skipping right along the surface of the water.

You scramble back into the cave as far as you can go, but the tunnel quickly narrows so you can't go any deeper. And the straggler is hoisting himself into the cave mouth, still gibbering. Your fingers curl around a rock, any rock, just some rock there on the ground, thank God, but then the straggler is upon you, snapping at you and gasping his fetid breath in your face, and you take that rock and smash smash SMASH it against his beautiful face until he falls back, shrieking and bloody.

The noise will draw the rest of the clan back. You need to finish this fast.

The straggler stumbles back to the creek, holding his bloody, ruined face in his hands, howling and blubbering. You scrabble forward, dropping out of the cave, and advance on him, the rock still clutched tight in your hand. You raise your rock and bring it down on the top of his head with a crack. The straggler falls into the shallow waters, face down. You bring the rock down again.

You don't stop until his head is a red pulp, the waters thick with brains and gore, until you're satisfied that there's no way he's getting back up. That's when you finally drop the rock and back away. Well. It's not like your situation could get any worse. It's not like you were ever going to talk things out amicably with the Hawkins clan. What's one more body?

Now what.

You need to get to Cat Hole. If you head upstream, you might be able to avoid leaving a trail for the hounds. It's the long way but it's safer. If you head into the woods…

You can cut directly up the ridge to Cat Hole. And, well, there's folks out there. Folks living in Bloodstump and Haintsville and The Pits who might help you. Probably not. Most folk probably don't wanna cross the Hawkins clan. But you never know. They might.

The woods are alive with the secret love songs of insects, but still for the sounds of people. The Hawkins boys must still be tracking you through the creek. Your leg is cramping but you have to keep going, dragging it along behind you.

The Hawkins boys are all out working the land and their mother... Well, you've never seen the Mrs. Hawkins. Presumably she's out doing chores as well. Pa's the only one home when you come calling. He has to stoop to extricate himself from the doorway and, when he stands up straight, he's at least 8 feet tall. His face is all beard.

There's a crucifix hanging in the door frame, reminding you that the Hawkins clan still follows the old god. No one else on the mountain does that. Them that come from Bloodstump follow the Dark Wanderer. Them that come from The Pits follow Poor Lazarus. Them that came from Cat Hole, when folk could come from Cat Hole, follow the Great Yowler. But the Hawkins clan has never thrived in towns. They've always lived apart and they've never taken kindly to visits from traveling preacher men. They don't take kindly to visits in general.

That's why it's so unusual that Pa Hawkins made you that offer.

"Reckon you thought on my offer," he says. He spits a wad of tobacco juice, but it just dribbles into his beard.

"Reckon I did."

He nods, and then he yells, "Priscilla! Priscilla, git your ass out here. The hog man wants ta see ya."

Priscilla is a slight girl, so slender and delicate that she looks like she might break in half at a breeze. She's absolutely swimming in her gingham dress. You wince when Pa Hawkins rests his enormous, hairy knuckles on her shoulder; it looks like the weight of his hand could crush her like a sparrow.

"This is th' hog man, Priscilla," says Pa Hawkins. He's

never bothered to learn your name in all your years of dealings. "You're gonna go with him."

Priscilla is as pale as fresh laundry, her voice quiet and shy. She's young, but her long, limp hair is a blinding snow white. Without another word, she walks to your side.

"Priscilla is our pride and joy," says Pa Hawkins. "The missus and I, well, we tried for so long for a daughter and all we got was sons. Starting to think we might never have another gal in the house, and I can tell you, that sorta thing just makes a woman ache inside when she don't have a daughter to pass on her woman ways. Beginnin' to think maybe there was something wrong with the wife's guts. But yessir, we persevered and now we got Priscilla here. We persevered. The good Lord rewards those that persevere, don't they?"

You nod politely. Pa Hawkins's talk of his weird religion makes you uncomfortable.

"You can have her, hog man, but you gotta treat her right. We don't cotton to no one treating our little Priscilla bad."

"I'll treat her right," you say.

"You best do that," says Pa Hawkins. "You got yers, now I git mine." He rubs his massive, meaty hands together in anticipation. "Let's see that hog."

The wind is whistling.

That whistling doesn't sound natural. What is that? You wish you had your shotgun, but you lost it in the chaos when the Hawkins boys surprised you in the middle of feeding the pigs. It's probably still at home, lying in the mud of the pig waller.

The whistling is louder now. Something in the tree reflects the moonlight and you look up.

Glass bottles hang from the tree branches, suspended by red yarn, gently bobbing in the breeze like chimes. The wind whistles softly as it plays over the mouths of the bottles. There are dozens of them hanging from every tree. Someone did this. Someone must live nearby.

There's a light ahead.

It's a cottage, raised off the forest floor on wooden stilts, the splintering shingles of its roof caked with a thick blanket of moss. More glass bottles hang suspended from the eaves by red yarn. You can see the guttering flames of candles through the grimy glass windows. The door has a sigil painted on it in red. You don't recognize the sigil, but you know what it means.

A witch woman lives here.

You approach the house, but you don't get close before you realize that you're not alone. A shape in the shadows of the front porch moves. You hear the click of a shotgun cocking.

"Don't move," says a raspy voice. "Old Mag sees ya. Don't move."

Old Mag moves out of the shadows, shotgun pointed straight at your brain. She isn't that old, you realize, as she moves into a shaft of moonlight. People probably call her 'old' because she's mostly bald, just a few wisps of long, white hair still clinging to her cranium, but from her face you'd estimate she can't be older than 50. She's fat, probably the fattest woman you've ever seen, with an enormous sagging gut and heavy tits. She's naked but for the necklaces of elk teeth around her neck and the bracelets and bangles around her wrists and ankles. The front porch creaks loudly at her every step.

She has one blue eye and one black eye.

She keeps the shotgun trained on your forehead. You raise your hands in the air, slowly, tentatively, to show you're safe.

"Hospitality!" you say. Old Mag is a witch woman, after all. She wouldn't betray her duty of hospitality. "The Hawkins boys are after me," you add, just to underscore the desperate nature of the situation.

She keeps her shotgun aimed, but you see a brief flicker of hesitation in her mismatched eyes.

"What did you do?" she asks.

"I killed one of the Hawkins boys," you say. "Just now."

"Bullshit, that wouldn't bring 'em all down from the mountain. They'd just make more. What did you *really* do?"

You pause. Old Mag is a witch woman, after all. She can help. "I took the Hawkins girl to be my wife," you say. "Pa Hawkins came to me with her; he wanted a hog in exchange. We made the trade and it's all fair and even."

"I heard about that," says Old Mag. "I seen your wife. I seen her out at night. You know about that?"

You don't respond.

"Ain't my business what folks do with their time," says Old Mag. "And certainly ain't no law says a woman can't be out at night. But what I seen..."

A sound from the woods sets your hair on end, but it's just the wind whistling through those bottles again. Nothing to worry about. Not yet.

"We did the trade," you repeat. "We did the trade, and she was mine. I ain't done nothing that wasn't my right. After what she did to me, I did what I needed to do."

Old Mag sucks in her breath between gapped, yellow teeth.

"Don't sound like the Hawkins boys see it that way," she says. "Or I reckon they wouldn't be after ya. And you don't cross them Hawkins. You know that, sure as you know these mountains. They'll find you. They'll find you and they'll kill you."

When you make to leave, Pa Hawkins hands you a small,

wooden chest. A tarnished nickel crucifix is shoved through the latch, holding it closed.

"Priscilla's dowry," says Pa Hawkins. "Mind you don't open it. It ain't fer you to see."

"What kind of dowry is that? I'm her husband!"

"It ain't fer you to see," repeats Pa Hawkins. "You open it and God help you, hog man. We'll find you and we'll kill you."

Is he joking? You're not sure. You decide that it's best not to pry. It's probably part of their weird religion, so it's easy enough to ignore. It's probably something that brings comfort to Priscilla in this time of change, and you're only too happy to do what you can to make your new wife comfortable.

You soon find that Priscilla doesn't talk much. She does her chores around the homestead without complaint and without difficulty; she slops the hogs and feeds the chickens and sweeps the floor and darns the socks and, at night, she climbs quietly but obediently into bed.

On the rare moments when there aren't chores to do—and those moments are indeed rare on the homestead—she sits and stares, unblinking, into the distance.

The dowry chest remains on a shelf above the stove, unopened.

Old Mag shoves a shallow plate of morels and ramps across the table toward you. In all the excitement, you didn't even realize you were hungry, but you're ravenous. You devour this meal gratefully as Old Mag settles her wide bottom onto the chair across the table from you. She lights her pipe and stares at you intently with her black eye.

The inside of the cottage, you realize, is dark but for the flickering light of the candles. You get the impression that the walls are lined with shelves, and the shelves are filled with jars. You get the impression that things are watching you from the jars.

"You can't stay here," says Old Mag suddenly. She sucks on her pipe with rapid, nervous gulps. "I done fulfilled my duty of hospitality," she says. "You ate your fill. Now you gotta get before them Hawkins boys find you. I don't want no trouble."

"There's a town up on the ridge, least there was," you say. "You know it? Cat Hole?"

She chews her pipe stem between big, flat teeth. "I know it."

"The church up there, that's consecrated ground. That's still good, right? The Hawkins follow the old god, so..."

"They'll find you and they'll kill you." She stands and clears the empty dish from the table. "But a church is as good a place to die as any, I reckon."

You loop around the old Indian trail and slip through the Needles and finally crest Fatback Ridge, your footsteps muffled as you trudge through mats of fallen pine needles. You reach the top without incident. At the ridge, you see a small roadside shrine—a little wooden box topped with a peaked roof—in the crook of a tree. Inside the box is what appears to have once been a small, plaster statue of the Virgin Mary, mother of the old god, but the head has been replaced with a cat skull.

That's when you see the first cat.

He's a massive, black tom sitting in the crook of an old elm tree, golden eyes shimmering in the moonlight. He's bigger than any cat you've ever seen before.

He bares his fangs, flattens his ears, and hisses. Then he drops from his perch and pads away into the night.

Further on, there's a rotten, wooden fence with a sign—DO NOT ENTER. BLOOD WORM QUARANTINE SITE. GREENBRIAR RIDGE COUNTY DEPARTMENT OF HEALTH—but you easily push it over and step into Cat Hole.

Cat Hole wasn't much when it was a town and it's even less now. The rotten frames still remain for a few buildings, but the only thing that hasn't completely fallen to ruin is the church. Cats of every size pad silently between the trees, and dozens more glowing eyes regard you from the shadows here.

This place is lousy with cats. The whole town smells of cat piss.

The old preacher tried to consecrate the church to the new gods when the blood worms messed up his head, but that's the thing about churches. You can't just...repurpose them. It's not like turning a barn into a shed or a shed into a barn. The land remembers.

Whatever that old preacher did, you can still feel the energy here, in the walls, in the beams.

And you reckon the Hawkins boys will feel it too, when they come.

The doors are ajar. You walk right in. You pull them shut behind you.

The church is mostly empty. Everything that can be looted has long since been looted, and the moonlight pours in through the big sucking holes in the ceiling left by years of wind and rain. Cats sit, watching you with big, yellow eyes from the shadows by the walls. The hissing and yowling is constant as they talk amongst themselves. They seem content to leave you be, at least for now. The reek of cat piss is even more overwhelming inside the church.

The floor of the church is a solid mat of dead cats, brittle and mummified, their tiny bones crackling as you step through them. There are still pews here, buried under mountains of cat hair and still more cat carcasses. The smashed altar is covered with small fetishes made of string and fabric. Someone has scrawled something across the back wall of the chancel in a language that you don't recognize.

You hear a mangled howl in the distance. The cats bristle and yowl in response.

Another howl. And a third. Definitely the Hawkins hounds. It was only a matter of time. They've found your scent again.

"Hog man!"

Shit. It's Pa Hawkins.

"Hog man! We know you're in there. Get your ass out here. Get out here and face us."

You don't say anything. You wait.

"We got you surrounded. I got my boys all around this church. You best get your ass out here and take yer medicine, you know what's good for ya."

You scoot toward the wall and peer through a crack in one of the smashed stained-glass windows. The Hawkins boys are all around the church. Some of them are holding torches. Some of them are carrying shotguns. Some of them are holding hounds at bay by their chains. The hounds are snapping and frothing, driven mad by the knowledge that their quarry is so near.

At an angle, you can see one man in the circle, backlit by torches, towering above the others. That must be Pa Hawkins.

"You know why we're here," he shouts. He spits a gob of chaw tobacco at the ground. Yeah. That's definitely Pa Hawkins. "I told ya, hog man, I told ya what we'd do if ya didn't treat Priscilla right. Now we found ya. We found ya and we're gonna kill ya."

You hold your breath. They're bluffing. They want you to come out, so they can do the deed off of consecrated ground. Everyone knows the Hawkins clan still follows the old god. They're afraid of his wrath. When you don't come out, you hear the Hawkins boys start to squabble amongst themselves. They don't like being so near the church.

"Ain't right, pa," one says. "Ain't right."

"Shut yer gob," says Pa. "Shut it."

"Ain't right, pa."

"Ain't right what th' hog man done to Priscilla," says Pa, drooling a fresh gusher of tobacco juice into his beard. "Now shut your gob and wait." He yells, "Hog man, this is it. You come out now."

You wait. They're not coming in.

But you forgot that dogs don't follow any god.

A Hawkins hound smashes through the stained-glass window, spilling shards over the church floor. It flops on the ground like a seal, barking and babbling and snapping its teeth at nothing. You scramble away as it staggers unsteadily to its feet. Its mouth goes almost all the way around its head. It breathes in big, wheezing snorts, clear liquid snot trailing from its flared nostrils, and every snort sounds more sure, more resolute as it slowly, gradually starts to block out the jumble of church smells—the cats, the piss, the remnants of an old religion, the tatters of a new one—and focus on one, single scent. Your scent. It's coming toward you.

A second crash. Another hound is inside the church. The cats scream. Cats are spilling out of the walls, shrieking and yowling. You could hope that the chaos of a thousand screaming, spitting cats might be enough to distract the Hawkins hounds, but they're all walking toward you, advancing on you, and there's nowhere to run.

The ground drops out from under you as the first hound leaps. In a brief moment of clarity, you wonder what will happen to your hogs without you to slop them.

Priscilla, you find, makes a fine wife. She fulfills all the duties that Pa Hawkins promised she would. She rises early, even earlier than you do, so that when you lurch out of bed, you find she's already frying grits for your breakfast. She remains behind to sweep the floors and mend the linen when you go out to milk the hogs. She's prepared you a lunch of squash pickles and beer mustard when you return. At dinner, there's rootmush and hog milk. On most nights, she continues to clean long after you've retired to bed. But on nights when you feel the need and you call for her, she comes.

She doesn't talk much, but, in all other things, she is proficient.

She makes a good wife. You can't say that she isn't a good wife.

whats the matter then

"You don't talk much," you say at dinner one night. She sits at the opposite end of the table, regarding you with big, lamp-like eyes. She hardly ever blinks. She's like a fish.

She asks you if she should talk more.

It's a good question. You know plenty of menfolk who can't get their wives to shut up. Plenty of menfolk can't stand to hear the chatter of women. Maybe it's for the best that she's so quiet. Maybe she's anticipating your needs and knows them better than you do, understanding that her silence will only make the bond between the two of you deeper.

"I guess not," you say. You stab at your food and wonder how Pa Hawkins tricked you because he must have.

That night, you awaken suddenly. Priscilla has her mouth on your cock.

She pauses as if she senses that you're awake. You lie still, keeping your breathing steady. Eventually, she resumes her work. She sucks and sucks and sucks, slurping the knob of your dick until it's purple and swollen and then twitching out ropes of semen. You bite your lips, hiding your reaction. She laps it up, slurp-slurp-slurp, like a little cat, her little, pink tongue lizard-licking up all the goo along the under-ridge of your frenulum, and she keeps licking long after your spent dick has withered back down to normal. She slides out of bed and drops to the floor. You hear her leave the room.

what the fuck

The next morning, you rise and find her preparing breakfast.

"Breakfast looks good," you say.

She says that she likes serving her husband.

The day passes as normal. That night you retire to bed. As usual, you fall asleep waiting for her.

You awaken in the night with her mouth on your cock again.

The third night is the same. But this is the night that you follow her.

She leaves the house. She's stepping nimbly through the brush, graceful as a deer, the moonlight silhouetting her slender body in relief against the filmy, white material of her nightgown. You follow at a distance, stepping as light as you can. When she pauses, you pause. When she continues, you continue.

She shimmies through the fence of the hog waller and slithers through the mud. The pigs start to stir, noticing a stranger among them. Grunting, they trot away as she passes, as if they know not to disturb her. She slides through the far fence and continues.

She's headed into the woods.

There's a clearing ahead where the moonlight falls upon the ground. Priscilla stops here. She falls to her knees and starts to dig, scratching frantically at the earth like a dog. Eventually, she has a hole.

She spits your seed into the hole.

Then she starts to yowl.

At first, it's just noises. She's mewling and crying like an animal, slapping the earth with her dirt-stained hands and kicking her heels up in the air. On her hands and knees, she gallops around the hole three time widdershins, still yowling the whole time.

You don't need to see anymore.

You know a love spell when you see one.

what the fuck

You stagger back to the house. The dowry chest is on a shelf above the stove. You smash the crucifix and bust open the chest.

You hear a piercing shriek from the woods, so high and shrill that a flock of nightjars rises from the trees and takes flight in panic. There's a change in the air, perhaps just the wind changing direction, perhaps something more. You suspect that Priscilla will not be returning. You have a sudden image of her lying collapsed, facedown in that hole, her love spell forever incomplete. You stopped her just in time.

Inside the box is another crucifix, metal, red with rust. There's also a mummified cock, shriveled and brittle, studded with rusty nails. And there's a note, scrawled in crabbed handwriting on a slice of folded, yellowed paper.

will find yoo & will kill yoo

WELL WISHERS

By April Yates

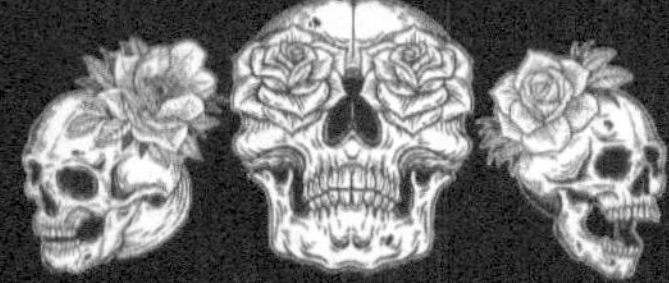

"Stop, someone might see," Payton said, even as she pulled Stevie closer, slipping a hand up the back of her T-shirt, nails digging lightly into firm flesh.

"It's okay." They'd ducked off the trail behind the remains of a stone wall. "There's no one around for miles."

Miles might have been an exaggeration, though the vast expanse of countryside made it feel that way. Payton and Stevie had been making their way across the Peak District from campsite to campsite on foot. Stevie had wanted to show Payton where she had grown up.

Payton—a city girl through and through—had taken to hiking across hills and fields remarkably well. Stevie had shown her stone circles and well dressings, explained the painstaking work of building a picture by pushing flowers and seeds into clay, only for it to wilt and crumble soon after. They had even visited the village of Eyam, where the people had selflessly quarantined themselves during the great plague.

"If we don't start walking again soon, we won't make it to the next site before those rain clouds catch up with us."

"Why don't we set up the tent here?" Stevie said. "You won't have to worry about being quiet all the way out here."

Payton pushed Stevie away with a laugh. "I want a shower and a proper, sit-down meal before I even so much as think about sex."

Stevie gave a mock whine of rejection before picking up her backpack. "Let's get you that shower then."

Stevie fished the ordnance survey map out, spent a moment squinting at it, looking intently at an oak tree before bringing the paper closer to her face.

"Is that helping?"

"No. I don't understand. Looking at this, it's as if we're on a completely different trail than the one we were on a few moments ago."

"You must be looking at the wrong grid." Payton said.

Stevie held the map out to her. "Have a look, but you see that tree?"

"You mean, before you dragged us behind that wall? And you probably didn't notice it before because you've only had one thing on your mind today."

The air was taking on the oppressive tone of an impending storm.

"It's a bloody big tree, Payton. I'd like to think even I'm not that tunnel-visioned." Stevie took Payton's hand and gave it a light squeeze. "We'll carry on along here, bound to come across something recognizable soon. We're only supposed to be 20 minutes away from the site."

They walked as grey clouds encroached ever closer.

A half-hour later and they were still walking, only now fat droplets of rain fell intermittently, a threat that at any moment the heavens would unleash themselves onto the earth in a torrent of rage.

Every few minutes, Payton checked her phone. Still no bars. Stevie wasn't having much luck the old-fashioned way either. The compass needle swung erratically, never settling.

The track they were following was well-worn, dirt and stone compacted tightly beneath their feet, suggesting it had to lead somewhere.

"Thank fuck for that!"

"What?" Payton asked, shocked from her reverie.

"That." Stevie pointed at the farmhouse, well-tended, lights on, warm and inviting. A perfect beacon of civilization.

Payton picked up the pace, the heavy feeling in her legs gone at the prospect of a soft chair and a cup of coffee.

As they approached the house, the rain came.

"Typical," Stevie muttered. "We'd have been inside in five minutes."

Through the torrent, a young woman was running to meet them. "What are you doing?" she asked briskly. "How did you find us?"

It had only taken a moment in the rain for the woman's clothes to become plastered to her. Payton noticed Stevie's eyes drift downwards. She gave her a gentle poke.

"To be honest, we're not sure on both counts," Stevie said. "We strayed from the trail a little, thought we'd got back on track, but must have got on a different one entirely."

"Does anyone know you're here? I mean, I wouldn't want you to just go home and leave the services looking for you in vain. You'd be surprised how many people do that. Waste resources and time through their own stupidity."

Payton laughed. "We couldn't get a signal to call for help."

The woman's eyes narrowed. "American?"

"Yes."

"We hate to impose on you," Stevie said, eager to hurry the conversation on and get them out of the rain, "but if we could come inside, just to get our bearings more than anything."

"Yes, of course," the woman looked beyond them, eyes

flitting across the horizon. "These summer storms never tend to last long."

The storm was still raging an hour later.

They sat in a kitchen dominated by an ancient, AGA stove next to which sat an equally ancient-looking woman, tissue paper-thin skin spread over sharp bones. The young woman had introduced herself as Jess, but had offered no name for the old woman.

During the time spent waiting for the storm to pass, Stevie and Payton were still not any closer to finding out where they were.

"I don't think this storm is going to pass any time soon," Jess said. "You could spend the night. The men will be back tomorrow with the Jeep; they'll take you anywhere you want to go."

Payton looked at Stevie, raising her eyebrows. It was a look that, said, *You hear that? The menfolk will be home soon!*

"Thank you," Stevie said, "that's very kind of you."

"I'll show you to your rooms." Jess got up. "There aren't many of us left, so we've plenty of them."

"We don't mind sharing."

"I used to hate sharing with my sister when I had one."

"Oh, we're not sisters, we're—" Stevie began

"Friends!" Payton quickly finished.

The old crone cackled. Jess allowed a tight-lipped smile. "Follow me."

They followed her up creaking stairs, each step sending dust motes up from the carpet. Once upstairs, Jess directed them to a room each, instructing them to leave their backpacks before showing them both the bathroom.

"I'll leave you two alone to clean up while I make something to eat."

Payton eyed the grimy tub with suspicion.

Stevie sidled up beside her. "You can have your shower now."

"I'm not getting in that thing."

Payton turned to the sink. Turning on the tap, she sighed with relief when she saw that the water ran clear.

"Why did you say we were just friends?" Stevie asked

"Because I have more than an ounce of self-preservation about me. I'm getting a weird vibe from this place. I don't know what their views are, and I'd rather not be kicked out in this weather."

"We have the tent."

"We'd be soaked through setting it up in this."

"If you'd taken my suggestion earlier, right now we'd be snuggled up close and you'd be wet in a good way."

"You're so Goddamn sure of yourself it's sickening, you know?"

"Yeah!" Stevie pulled Payton to her, placing a kiss on her neck, "but that's what makes me so adorable."

"I suppose we better go back down. I don't know how I'm going to last an evening in such fun company as theirs."

"We'll have an early night. I don't think we'll be lying when we say we're bone tired."

Still the storm raged on, the wind whipping the rain so hard against the glass it rattled in its frames. Stevie had never known anything like it in this part of the world. There was no way they could have lasted the night in their small tent. It would be torn apart in this weather, even if they could get it up in the first place.

The meal that Jess had prepared was far too heavy and stodgy for a summer's evening. A stew of vegetables and what Stevie could only hope was beef, it had been cooking for so long the potatoes had disintegrated and all the moisture had leached from the meat, leaving tasteless chunks that were hard to swallow.

Not so hard to swallow as the conversation, mind. Jess and her grandmother were, in short, crazy.

Stevie had assumed the brand of crazy was the garden-variety Christian. They had bowed their heads before their meal and Stevie had braced herself for mentions of Jesus and the Lord's name. Instead, the prayer was one of guttural sounds. Stevie glanced over at Payton. She had studied language and linguistics at university. The narrowing of her eyes told Stevie that the tongue they were speaking was not one Payton recognized.

"It must be nice, living out here. When the weather isn't so bad, that is."

Payton turned her fork over and over between her fingers as she spoke. Stevie placed her hand on Payton's bare thigh and gave it a reassuring squeeze. Payton put the fork down next to the nearly full bowl and declared, with a little too much exuberance, that it was lovely.

Jess looked at the cold, congealed mess in front of Payton for a moment, before picking it up and setting it down next to the sink with a heavy clatter.

"Thank you so much for your hospitality," Stevie said. "It's been much appreciated. After we've helped you with the dishes, me and Payton will get out of your hair."

The briefest of glances from Jess to grandmother, who gave a curt nod in return. "No, you're our guests after all. I'll clean up. Then I think it's probably time we went to bed as well. Give me five minutes and I'll make sure you're settled in."

In separate beds, Stevie thought.

It was a lot longer than five minutes for Jess to clean up with her refusing all offers of help. Stevie and Payton had no choice but to sit waiting at the table. Eventually, Jess led them up the stairs before pointing them to their separate rooms.

"She suffers from night terrors, my grandmother. It's best if you just ignore anything strange you hear."

They nodded in solemn silence before departing for their beds.

Stevie couldn't tell if there were any strange noises in the house, mainly because of the noise of the storm outside.

She waited half an hour before creeping across to Payton's room. Before she even opened the door, Stevie knew Payton was asleep. She could tell by the soft, snuffling snore coming from within. A snore that Payton patently denied having. Stevie padded into the room and sat on the edge of the bed. The ancient springs squealed and sank beneath their combined weight.

Payton woke with a start.

"What—?"

She put her lips to Payton's, silencing her but for the slight moan of desire that escaped her.

Stevie crawled in next to her, the limited space crushing their bodies close.

"It's like being a teenager again," Payton whispered, between kisses, "like at any moment they could come busting in."

"You better be quiet then."

Stevie positioned herself onto her side, so that she could trail her hand up Payton's bare thigh before settling her hand lightly between her legs. Payton raised her hips up, desperate for more pressure.

Stevie was just about to kiss Payton again when, with the crack of wood snapping, Payton was deposited on the floor. Stevie peered over the edge of the bed, eyes wide in the darkness.

"Are you?" She tried, and failed, to suppress a giggle. "Are you alright? So much for trying to be quiet."

Stevie scrabbled out of the lopsided bed, nearly tripping over herself in the process. Turning the light on, she saw Payton, still on the floor, sucking air through her teeth.

Stevie's amusement instantly ceased as concern kicked in.

"Oh, babe," she said, taking Payton's forearm, gently turning it this way and that, examining it. "I don't think it's anything too serious. I think you've just knocked it."

"Well, thank you, Doctor Stevie—" Payton's eyes darted to the window.

"What—?"

Payton brought her good hand up to Stevie's mouth, gesturing towards the window with her chin. The same guttural language that Jess and her grandmother had spoken at dinner carried on the air, mingled with the sounds at the storm. Stevie turned the light back out and went to the window. Payton followed her.

"Can you see anything?" Payton whispered.

Stevie had to admit there wasn't much she could see beyond a sky bruised purple and flecked with lightning.

"Can you see anything?" Payton repeated.

"No, but I've never seen a sky like this."

The only sounds now were the pelting of rain against glass and their breathing, punctuated by the rumble of thunder. Stevie was just about to suggest going back to her room when a flash of lightning illuminated the old woman standing outside, arms outstretched towards the sky. The white nightgown plastered to her body showed every frail, jutting bone. Stevie shuddered in sympathy.

"The old girl must have dementia," Stevie said, shoving her feet into Payton's hiking boots and grabbing her coat. "I'll find Jess and help her get her in."

Stevie went into the hallway. She had no idea which room was Jess's, so just started calling her name.

No answer.

"Jess?"

Maybe she was already outside? Stevie hurried down the stairs, taking the last two in one jump.

She rounded the corner into the kitchen and slammed into Jess, who was holding a soaked grandmother by the arm. She blinked blankly at Stevie.

"Night terrors," she said, steering the woman past her and up the stairs.

Stevie lingered a moment, staring out the window at the continuing rain, before going back upstairs.

She found Payton in her room, sitting on the bed.

"I was getting worried."

"I've only been gone five minutes," Stevie said, kicking off Payton's boots.

"No, it's been much longer than that. I saw Jess out there with the old woman."

"Yeah, she was bringing her in."

"No, she was already out there before you left. Her arms were in the air like she was at a damn revival meeting. I'm scared."

"It's one woman and an old lady. What could they possibly

do?"

"You didn't see them both."

Stevie shifted the small armchair from the corner of the room in front of the door.

"I don't know how much use that's going to be," Payton snapped.

"True, I don't think it'll stop anyone getting in. But I'll hear them."

"I know it seems silly."

"It's not silly," Stevie said, enveloping her in a hug. "As soon as it's light, we'll be gone."

Payton's sleep was fitful, her eyes never leaving the door.

Sunrise was 4:40am, the longest day of the year. Payton shook Stevie awake. She squinted against the powerful ray of light that flooded in, unimpeded by the threadbare curtains.

"Let's go."

They dressed quickly and made their way downstairs.

"Hopefully, they aren't up yet," Payton whispered. They made it to the front door.

Locked.

Stevie hunted around on the sideboard for the keys.

"Let's just go out the back," Payton said nervously.

Stevie spent a few more minutes rummaging through the drawers before relenting.

The kitchen was full. Jess and grandmother, along with the menfolk they had spoken of last night.

"Good morning," one of the men said, raising his spoon in greeting.

"Morning," Stevie said, trying to equal the brightness of his tone. She couldn't help thinking that the sun seemed too bright for five o'clock in the morning. "Jess, thank you for letting us into your home. We won't bother you any longer."

One man stood imposingly by the kitchen door.

"We can't let you go on an empty stomach," the old woman said.

She indicated the two empty chairs at the table for Stevie and Payton to sit.

They sat.

"Today's one of the few days we have fresh fruit. Do you know how painful the want is when you're denied something as simple as a strawberry? What it's like to not be able to go beyond the property line?" Her eyes hardened. "I've been tethered here for decades. I thought that only those of my blood could make it through the veil. Over the years they've dwindled away. That or they simply choose not to visit." A pointed look here at one man, who tried to avert his eyes. "Those who do come bring me a bounty. But never have I had such a gift bestowed upon me as fine as you two."

The old woman rose from her seat. There was a newfound plumpness to her that filled the wrinkles in her face.

"Frank, will you escort our guests outside?"

Frank gave a grimace in response, draining his cup before slamming it down on the table.

"Stevie, Payton, would you mind following Frank, or will he need to persuade you?"

Stevie looked at Frank's hands, massive and calloused. Working hands. When they'd been wrapped around his mug, there was not a speck of the ceramic to be seen. Stevie thought about how easily those hands could wrap around Payton's neck.

"Fine, we'll go. Just don't touch her!"

The old woman nodded, and the man stepped back. They went out into the already stifling day.

The old woman had not been exaggerating. The back garden had turned into a bounty. Bushels of flowers and fruits littered makeshift tables. Throngs of people moved between them, picking the choicest blooms. A young man with a tank strapped to his back walked up and down, misting them with water to prevent them wilting in the heat.

Stevie felt a slight pressure on her back, the old woman moving her forward. Beyond the crowds of people—mainly women, Stevie noticed—five wooden frames full of wet clay lay on the ground. Two of the five were empty. Work had begun on the other two. Three women knelt beside each frame, placing flowers and seeds into the soft clay. As they drew closer to the women's work, Stevie's blood ran cold.

Pushed deep within the clay of each frame was a woman. Their pale skin shimmered like ivory so they resembled cameo brooches. One was still alive, her breathing growing shallower with each new bloom that was placed. It was macabrely beautiful, the swirl of color and fragrance built around young, firm flesh.

"It's fortunate that we had so much extra this year. We really weren't expecting you two. But if the lord sees fit to give us this extra bounty…" The old woman clicked her fingers and four men appeared, two either side of Stevie and Payton, and took hold of their wrists. "Who are we to refuse?"

Stevie struggled against them. She didn't care about herself, but the whine of pain from Payton was a dagger through her heart. Payton's cries were growing in intensity, her breath hitching in her chest.

"Leave her alone!" Stevie cried.

"Take her, not me!"

Stevie fell still, utterly flabbergasted as to what she had just heard.

The old woman smiled. "It didn't take you long to turn. And why is it I should spare you?"

Stevie could practically see the cogs turning in Payton's head.

"If you let me go, I'll bring you someone every year." Payton paused a moment, gauging the old woman's reaction. "For ten years."

She hobbled over to Payton. "Ten years, girl. Every summer solstice, you need to bring me someone, and don't think you can go home to America and not pay me my dues."

"I won't, I promise," Payton said hurriedly, nodding with the enthusiasm of a car dash ornament.

"You bitch…" Stevie didn't have the energy to be angry. She could only muster up the facts. "You complete and utter bitch."

To her credit, Payton didn't try to justify herself or to apologize. Her resolution to stick to a decision was the one thing Stevie could still respect about her. They released Payton from her bondage as they pushed Stevie towards the crowd of waiting women. Deft fingers quickly undressed her, her skin prickling under the sun almost instantly, and Stevie wondered once again how it could be this bright and hot so early in the morning.

"You're so lucky," one woman whispered in Stevie's ear.

"I'm perfectly willing to swap places," Stevie whispered back. "I really don't mind."

The woman gave a serene smile in return.

"Yeah, I didn't think so," Stevie muttered.

They grabbed Stevie by the wrists and ankles, placing her down into the center of the frame. After the heat of the sun, the clay was cool and soothing. Calm enveloped Stevie, made ever greater by each flower the women lovingly pressed into the clay. She wanted to close her eyes, to drift off into oblivion. She just wished the last thing she saw wasn't Payton standing over her, whispering, "I'm sorry."

Again, and again, and again.

ALDERGROVE

By E.S. Corble

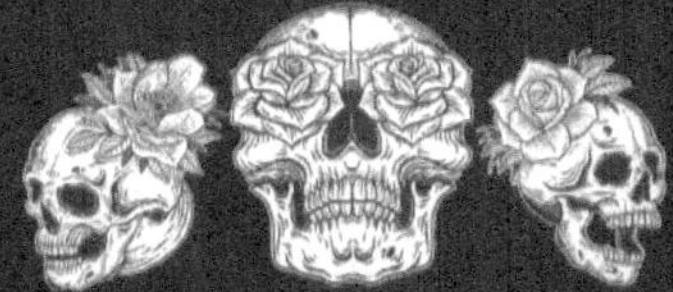

Aldergrove was crumbling.

From its silty soil to the cracked stained glass in its tower rooms, the town—if you could call it that—crumbled. Everywhere you looked were magpies, pecking at the harvest crops, knocking slates from the roofs and, all-in-all, devouring the crumbling town in a whirl of black and white feathers.

That's what Hetty thought as she passed through the strange wickerwood gates at the woods' edge, shuddering as the car started up the winding hill road.

"Why not just use metal?" she grumbled to herself. "Everyone else does!"

Hetty hadn't wanted to come to Aldergrove. She never had.

She was seventeen for a start. And Aldergrove, population of six hundred, was filled with crumbling people. She could see them through the window, and though the trees were marked with Autumn—a crumbling season—the people were lit in their own private sun, illuminating their wrinkled faces and flyaway hair from within.

There were no children in Aldergrove. Not today.

Yes. Aldergrove was a crumbling town filled with

crumbling people. Hetty scowled and slumped further down in her seat.

She hated this fucking island.

"Is this right?" the driver asked. "Seventy-Three Addles Avenue?"

Hetty looked out of the window and sighed.

"Yeah, this is it. Thank you."

'It' was a tall, narrow building in a line of tall, narrow buildings. What separated 73 Addles Avenue from the rest of Aldergrove's rinky-dink, white, picketed rows was a crimson rose bush growing before the door. Three mangy magpies were perched on the fence and flew off as the car drew to a stop.

Three for a girl. That must be me.

Hetty caught a glimpse of their eyes as they flew away. They were golden.

Later, as Hetty unpacked in the attic room, she felt no sense of relief. The one clear pane in the distended window frame looked up at the spiraling houses and the huge, carved stone that pinned the town to the hill on which it was built.

She poked her tongue out at Aldergrove.

It had been an afternoon just as she had dreaded it.

Her great aunt, Agnes, had thrown the door wide and the overwhelming scent of musk, roses and talc poured out in a wave. Coasting on top of the wave was the delighted cry of, "Henrietta!"

Great Aunt Agnes had changed so much since moving to Aldergrove. When Hetty was a little girl, she remembered her great aunt as a hard woman, all sharp edges and scowls in her dark dress suits. But Aldergrove had crumbled her away.

This Agnes was softened.

Her hair, once scraped into a tight bun, now hung in a white cloud around her head and her sharp features had grown soft and filled with foreign smile lines. Her eyes, once like flecks of flint, now looked odd, like eiderdown in her sockets. The dark suits had been replaced by loose cream—

robes

—clothing. Hetty missed the old Agnes. The woman who bustled her excitedly into the house, chirping about the upcoming festival and feast, was a stranger.

There was tea. Muffins, scones and sickly-sweet honey from the Aldergrove hives. Hetty discreetly spat hers into a napkin while Agnes spouted all the things you'd expect a distant and long-distance relative to say.

"You've grown so much!"

Yeah, you've changed too much.

"How are your parents?"

Angry with me.

"How is school"

Bad and you know it. I didn't get sent here for nothing.

Agnes sipped her tea and smiled fondly over the saucer at Hetty.

"I hope you have a good stay. It's important that you stay within the Aldergrove walls though. The woods beyond are wild, and not like the woods on the mainland. The harvest festival is in a few days, and I've already made you a magpie mask for the festivities!"

With delight, she held aloft a hodge-podge mask of dark feathers and near-black leaves. A sharp clay beak leered out at Hetty. It looked slick and greasy in the lamplight and smelt sick, like something long-since rotten.

"Do you like it?"

Hetty forced a smile to her face, not wanting to seem rude, especially when Agnes' eyes were that excited...and something else. For a moment, Hetty could have sworn that Agnes's eyes flashed a deep gold, and that when they did it was like something not-Agnes peered out from behind them. The room felt colder and the smell of earth permeated the air. Then as fast as it was there, it was gone.

"It's lovely," Hetty said, through her teeth.

She was half-certain that Agnes could hear her heartbeat.

Night fell quickly over Aldergrove.

From the window in the attic, the rooftops of Aldergrove seethed in a sea of black feathers, lit dimly by the light from other distant windows. The cawing was deafening, and Hetty dreaded the prospect of trying to count the endless tide of magpies. She shut the curtains and turned on her phone, trying to drown out the rhyme that had been told at her cribside before school started and everything began to rust and wither.

"One for sorrow,
Two for joy,
Three for a girl,
Four for a boy,
Five for silver,
Six for gold,
Seven for a secret never to be told.
Eight for a wish,
Nine for a kiss,
Ten a surprise you should be careful not to miss,
Eleven for health,
Twelve for wealth,
Thirteen beware, it's the devil himself."

Thirteen-by-thirteen-by-thirteen sounds about right for Aldergrove, she thought bitterly.

Her phone offered no solace. There was no cell service in Aldergrove. Just another stupid, crumbly thing about the hill town. Hetty swore quietly to herself as she turned her phone off and tried to get comfy on the lumpy bed. It wasn't like she needed her friends anyway. They weren't there for her on the mainland; why would they be there for her here?

Sleep crashed over her.

The carriage ahead of her wailed and howled, low, echoing distantly down the darkened train. The doors rattled and thudded, the shrill sound of scraping metal growing in pitch as the screams died down into something croaky, something almost...cacophonous.

Then silence. Slowly, the doors creaked open, and a tidal wave of iridescent darkness spilled into the carriage, smothering all in its wake.

The sun stung Hetty's eyes the next day, and she cursed the nightmare of the previous night. She hadn't been able to go back to sleep after it woke her up, fighting for air in the darkness of the attic, darkness that felt for a moment—just a moment—like feathers.

In the afternoon sun, she shivered.

All around her, the people of Aldergrove chattered excitedly in their pale clothes, peering up at the carved stone in the town's center. The alder trees surrounding it swayed softly, a chorus of whispers that masked the hissing of the woods surrounding the town.

It's like we are in a sea of trees...and the hill is a crumbling rock.

Agnes squealed happily beside her, shaking her arm with glee.

"Oh, it's so exciting, Henrietta! You're so lucky to be here for the third-year festival. Those are always really special."

Hetty rolled her eyes. She could see old men and women joining hands and circling round the standing stone, laughing in delight, the tones harsh and discordant like the magpies that circled overhead so fast Hetty couldn't count them.

Through the crowd of white clothes and dark feathers, she

spotted something red. Another teenager in a red hood stood near the crowd's edge like a drop of blood in the crowd. They looked exhausted, holding onto one of the trees for support.

Agnes noticed Hetty looking and her smile fell into something grim.

"Oh, you've spotted Kurban. Poor mite, his parents sent him to stay with his grandfather for a bit."

"What, did he get in trouble too?"

"No, no… There's some unpleasantness in the next town over and I daresay more children will be sent here." She brightened suddenly "But that means more people for the festival! Go see him, see if his grandfather has made him a mask yet."

Hetty was already going. She'd take a gloomy kid over Agnes any day.

The closer she got to Kurban, the odder she noticed he was. His eyes were tired and pinched, and his lower lip was red raw from being bitten, as were his nails. He spotted Hetty coming through the crowd and gave her an anxious smile.

"You a mainlander?"

"Yeah. You bored?"

"Well, it's better than town right now," he said, nodding his head forestward.

If Hetty squinted she could make out another town half-swallowed by trees, eerily quiet in the distance.

In fact, everything had gone eerily quiet. The crowd had turned towards the stone and stood silent, staring up at the tip. Three colossal magpies had landed there, and they surveyed the crowd with what seemed like cold indifference.

All Hetty's hair stood on end. There was something wrong about those birds, something intelligent about the way they stood stock-still.

"Three."

The word rippled through the crowd with reverence, soft and almost hissing.

No sooner had it died down than the magpies began to caw. Once, in unison. Then thrice, and another four, all while Aldergrove stared up in slack-jawed adoration. Finally, the magpies puffed their feathers out and—

bowed?

—before they flew back into the trees. Aldergrove was silent for a second. Then, there was a great cheer, and music began to play as the town erupted into dance around Hetty and Kurban.

"What just happened?" Hetty asked Kurban.

The boy shrugged.

"Aldergrove keeps its secrets, but knowing them, it's probably how many prunes people have to chew at the feast. We call them 'The Cult of the Grey Socks' over in town." He shot her another small smile that fell surprisingly fast. "Then again...stranger things have happened."

The day whiled away fast, and though she wouldn't admit it to herself, Hetty was enjoying the festival. The elation was infectious, and it pulled at her mouth like a set of hooks.

The sun set on crumbling Aldergrove, casting the town in red. The air turned cold and bit the bones of the teenagers under the alder tree, a taste of winter and a reminder that all things are harvested eventually.

After, Agnes emerged from the crowd, cheeks flushed red and cast in the light of the dull, red lanterns that were being lit around the stone and banquet table, casting long seething shadows across the floor.

"She the batty one?" Kurban asked, nudging Hetty.

Hetty raised an eyebrow as Agnes swayed towards them like a scarecrow given life. Her arms hung at her sides, grotesquely long in the red light, as though they had been dislocated. A low giggle slipped from her mouth as she made her way over, and the sickly smell of sweetened wine drifted on the breeze.

Hetty turned to Kurban and just nodded. That wasn't the

Agnes she knew.

"It's feasting time, you two." she slurred, her mouth stretching into a thin smile. "Come on, everyone's getting together for the decision. Oh, you're so lucky to be here. Youth are favored."

Her eyes glinted in the low light as she beckoned for the teenagers to follow and swayed towards the banquet table set up in the town center.

"What does she mean, 'Youth are favored'?" Hetty whispered to Kurban as they made their way over. The phrase skittered along her spine in a way she couldn't explain. After all, she and Kurban were the only ones there that could be remotely considered 'youth'.

"I dunno." Kurban muttered. "Is it just me or does something feel...off?"

Hetty's stomach growled.

"If the food is bad, do you wanna ditch and sneak off into the woods?"

Kurban went pale and froze in his tracks. After a moment, he shrugged and let out a strained laugh.

"Sure. Easily better than the Cult of the Grey Socks."

As they went, Agnes pulled a magpie mask low over her face and offered Hetty the one Hetty had made a point of leaving in the attic. A glance at the banquet table revealed that the entire town was masked with dark feathers and curved beaks.

Creepy.

She put on the slick, oily mask and shuddered, the smell of decay strong in her nose. Out of the corner of her eye, she saw that Kurban had one as well, and the distasteful curl of his mouth told her he felt the same way about it.

The banquet table was piled high with fresh produce, and meat so rare it bled onto the wooden platters. Pitchers of wine were scattered up and down the table, and at its center sat a wizened, old man with pale-blue vulture eyes.

Hetty didn't recall seeing him at the earlier festivities. He wore the same cream garments as the rest of Aldergrove, but his sharp face was shadowed over with a headdress of alder leaves and magpie feathers. His spindly hands clutched a bit of paper, and he leered down his nose at Hetty and Kurban as they sat opposite him.

Hetty glared back. She didn't much care for the look the old man was giving her.

He raised his chalice to her and drank deep.

The table quietened down immediately as all eyes turned to the old man, silence punctured only by the distant caw of magpies. Wine dripped down his pointed chin, his scraggly beard rejecting the liquid. With a rustle, two magpies swooped down and sat on his chair.

I thought magpies slept at night, Hetty thought to herself. *Are they trained?*

The old man finished his vessel, and everyone else at the table raised theirs. Agnes nudged Hetty sharply and Hetty raised the goblet to her lips.

The wine was sickly sweet, like drinking liquid sugar, and it clung to her teeth and throat like tar. She screwed her eyes shut until she heard everyone else slam their vessels back on the table and followed suit, spluttering in the cold night air.

Her head swam, the faces at the table looked distorted in the low red light.

The old man stood solemnly and opened his arms to the table.

"Alder's Grove. It has been a long year, hasn't it? From the deep snows of winter to the scorching summer sun, the elements have challenged us at every turn. We have some new faces, but they can never replace those few that we have lost."

Hetty looked around confused as many people nodded, one old lady openly weeping into her handkerchief.

"And I fear the year coming may be harder still. Already the seeds of discord have sprouted in neighboring towns, as this young boy could tell you—" He pointed across at Kurban, who jolted violently. "—and it will not be long before they come to our hallowed hill. This is why, this year, three must go beneath. To ensure our safety, our longevity, and our way of life."

Hetty's head was full of sweet fog, but the old man's words pierced through. Her blood ran cold and icy in her veins. She stopped breathing.

Beneath! What does he mean, beneath?

"Three beneath..." Aldergrove chanted, low and rumbling like distant thunder.

"It is a privilege to be chosen," the old man continued. "The first has already been selected, before our festivities began: Elder Fisher."

Hetty felt Kurban freeze beside her, and out of the corner of her eye saw he had turned a sallow grey. His hand shot out, seized hers, and squeezed tightly. She squeezed back.

"Elder Fisher has been with us for the last three decades and has very much earned the honor of being chosen from the pool of volunteers. To Elder Fisher, everyone. May his journey beneath be smooth and enlightening."

"Elder Fisher."

Another collective drink from the sickly-sweet wine.

"Now, with your blessing, Elder Fisher, I would like to announce the name of our second selection."

The masked man—Elder Fisher—beside the speaker nodded enthusiastically, his mask's beak spraying the table with more sweetened wine.

"Very well. This selection comes from outside Alder's Grove walls, but their blood runs deep here. I have conferred with the council, and we feel that the best selection to ensure safety from the dangers of this winter is the one who brings it with them. Kurban Fisher, my dear boy, you can join your grandfather on his journey."

A cheer rose around the table, but Hetty didn't hear it for the roar of blood in her ears. Her hands felt numb, barely registering Kurban letting go. She didn't breathe, nor move, not even to tear her eyes away from the two magpies on the Old Man's chair. Their eyes were glowing golden.

I've got to get out of here. What happens when someone is sent 'beneath'? Will they crumble? Will I crumble?

Her bones felt brittle as she turned to look at the now-empty seat where Kurban had sat. Some of the Aldergrove people had moved from the table and, with dull eyes, she watched the blurred figures tackle a running boy, tackle him amid a swarm of magpies.

Gotta get outta here...

Swaying, she stood, and her stomach cramped with nausea. What was in that wine? The red air swam and swayed, the floor coming up to meet her, cold grass in her nose and—

In her mind's eye, she saw it. The thing under the hill. The Alder. Just for half a heartbeat. And for a quiet moment, she was certain that he saw her too.

She woke with a gasp on Agnes' sofa.

"Henrietta? Sweetie, you fainted. Are you feeling alright?"

Agnes, still in her robes—oh, they were definitely robes—and mask, sat on the chair opposite the sofa, head tilted in concern. In her hands was a damp cloth and her fingers looked red at the tips, as though coated in blood.

"You were out during the feast, but I saved you some fruits as well."

Hetty didn't say anything, just stared at the person who

was no longer her great aunt. She was a stranger her family used to know. Aldergrove crumbled her from the inside and stuffed her full of feathers and leaves.

"Wha— What does going beneath mean?" Hetty asked, so quietly she wasn't sure she spoke.

"Oh, sweetling," Agnes said. Her voice was grating in the gloom, and Hetty wasn't sure if it was the wine, but it looked like Agnes's eyes shone gold in the magpie mask.

She locked eyes with Agnes, and slowly began to reach for the teapot under the table.

"Going beneath isn't what you think it is... Our Alder, he looks after us. He makes us well, keeps us safe, and we give gifts in return. Tokens of appreciation, and those tokens are blessed, for they get to live with him under the hill, in his home. I've been here for twenty years and not once has Alder harmed any tribute. He just changes them a little. That's all. It's an honor to be chosen by him. In fact, you—"

A little further...yes!

Hetty's hand closed around the teapot, and before Agnes could do anything, Hetty swung it hard into the side of her head, the shock of the impact travelling up her arm as the thing that was not her great aunt hit the floor and hissed.

She didn't stay to see what happened.

Hetty charged outside into the pitch-black street and rushed up the hill, the wind whistling in her ears as she went.

Aldergrove was eerily quiet, just the distant caw of magpies left to puncture the night air. Hetty paused by the ring of alder trees, clutching her ribs as she wrestled for air. A branch snapped near her, and she whipped her head around, just to be met with more darkness. Where was everyone?

Past the trees, the town center was still bathed in the red light of the lanterns. There was a cage beside the stone, ornate and twined with flowers. Inside the cage...

Kurban!

Hetty crept closer, aware now of each sound her shoes

made on the cobblestones, and just how chill the night was. The hair on the back of her neck prickled. She was being watched. She had to hurry.

She darted over to the cage as quietly as she could. Kurban was curled up in a ball, the space around him strewn with fresh produce, children's drawings and more flowers. The cage door was fastened with a large padlock, and Hetty wished she'd brought the teapot with her so she could perhaps smash it off.

"Kurban," she whispered. "Kurban, I've come to get you, we have to get out of here."

The boy stirred and sat up, his hand clasped over his head and a groan issuing from his lips.

"Hetty? What are you doing here?"

"I've come to get you! We have to go!"

He squinted at her in the low light, his eyes deeply bloodshot.

"Go where?"

"Away. Anywhere. Why don't you lead us over to your town? It's just across the wood, right?"

Around them, slips of shadow were landing silently, rustling their feathers soundlessly, closing in around the cage.

"You'll never make it at night," Kurban said softly "These woods are not mainland woods... I can't leave. I have to go with my Grampa."

"What the fuck are you talking about?"

Kurban shook his head, hiding his face in his hands. Hetty glanced over her shoulder, heart pounding. There were more magpies, watching them silently. Thirteen in all.

"My sister. My sister is gone. And they told me that, if I go with Grampa, they'll make sure it doesn't happen to anyone else, that if I go willingly no one else on the island will have to lose anyone. I... I want to go. I want to help. I don't know what will happen, but I don't want to let my family down."

"Don't be stupid! This is a fucking nightmare!"

"It's worse outside."

The magpies were creeping closer.

"Fine!" Hetty growled "If you want to stay here and die, then stay. I'm fucking leaving, and if I can, I'll send help, but I'm getting out of here!"

Hetty stood up and turned to head down the hill. The Magpies had encircled them and were now cawing angrily. Hetty saw red. She lashed out.

"Wait!"

But it was too late. Her foot had connected with the bird, and it was knocked back to the empty table with a squawk, the other magpies scattering back to the trees. There was silence.

"Hetty," Kurban moaned "You shouldn't have done that..."

Hetty balled her hands into fists and was stopped in her tracks by what she saw out of the corner of her eye.

The magpie was...changing.

The feathers were crumbling away like dust and ash, a long, spindly body unfurling as if from a cocoon. It was pale and thin, each rib countable, and mottled with green splotches. Feathers clung to the back of its arms and a pointed, human jaw slipped out from under the beak, like something wearing a magpie costume.

Hetty froze, eyes pinned to the creature as it spat a mouthful of black blood onto the cobblestone and smiled a carrion smile at her. A low laugh echoed in her head, bouncing across her skull, and she knew it belonged to the thing that had never been a magpie.

"RUN!" Kurban yelled, and Hetty snapped out of it.

The wind and branches whipped her cheeks as she ran, too fast for her feet to keep up. The hill spurred her speed, and around her in the darkness she heard more creatures laughing, their voices grating like glass on bone.

Shit, how far is it to Kurban's town? Can I outrun these things?

As she ran, she noticed lights flickering on in the houses

behind her, but it wasn't long before the wicker gate loomed out of the shadows, two red lamps flanking the gates to the woods beyond. To freedom.

Something slammed into her leg and she fell, a scream ripping from her throat. The creature was biting deep into her calf, and its talons sunk into the flesh. Before she could move, others landed on her arm, her belly, her head.

"LET ME GO!" Hetty screamed, writhing under the weight of the not-magpies.

The air went cold, and something hissed through the air, something cold and old, and Hetty screamed again, electric fear snaking up her spine.

Father... Father, we have chosen our third...

The thing on her head leaned down, the stink of rot and sour earth rolling off it. It bit into her ear and Hetty was swallowed by darkness.

There were drums. The rustling of trees, and the soft flow of a distant river. Hetty smelt smoke and honey. Chanting drifted on the air, the cawing of magpies and not-magpies puncturing the chant with short sharp bursts.

Hetty ached all over, and something dug into her wrists and ankles as everything drifted back into sight. She was in the cage.

Oh no... Oh, shit!

"You awake now?" Kurban muttered from beside her. "I told you, you shouldn't have done that."

"Get me out of here, Kurban!"

"Shush!" Elder Fisher snapped from outside the cage.

Hetty sat up and saw fully where they were.

It was a clearing at the base of the hill, ringed by alder trees and endless woods beyond, hemming them tightly into the clearing. The people of Aldergrove clustered around the cage holding the two teenagers, and they chanted and sang to the door carved into the hillside, flanked by two stones, flowers, harvest vegetables and prime beasts, ready for roasting. The not-magpies were perched on the roots of the colossal alder tree that shot out above the door.

Agnes stood beside Elder Fisher and smiled at Hetty, in spite of the blood caked along the side of her face and the bruising across her temple.

"Isn't it exciting?" she asked.

Hetty went cold. This had to be a dream. This couldn't be real.

A crunching rumble echoed through the clearing and Aldergrove let out a great cheer. Hetty found Kurban holding her hand again, in spite of the twine that bound them. She squeezed him tight, unable to rip her eyes away from what she saw.

The door was crumbling away. A deep, cavernous space opened beyond the arch formed by the roots, and from it came a growling and a stomp that shook the clearing.

"He's here!" someone in the crowd cried out in ecstasy. "The Alder is here!"

An echoing hum emanated from the tunnel, and Hetty screeched as she felt an unseen thing wrap itself around her brain but...

Then she wasn't scared anymore.

It was like being plunged into tepid water, floating across its surface in a sea of stars. And drifting under the tide, like whale-song, a voice. It made her smile.

What have you brought me this harvest, my littlings? Have you brought what I asked of you, my dear ones?

"Yes! Yes, Father Alder!"

From the tunnel, a figure emerged, carrying with it the low, ripe smell of deep wood and stagnant water. Its flesh seethed with roots, and branches sprouted from its head, autumn and summer leaves cresting the twigs. There was no face, but there were hunks of amber that shone from within, a golden light which lit the clearing in an unearthly glow.

The Alder turned, creaking, to the three humans across from it, two caged and one uncaged.

Perfect. You have done well, my littlings. One for wisdom, one for self-sacrifice, and one for self-preservation. They will serve our hill well for the year to come.

The Alder raised a twisted hand and with a howl, Elder Fisher fell to the floor and writhed as he began to change.

Hetty watched dreamily as Elder Fisher shrank, and pinfeathers burst through his skin with a sharp popping sound. His clothes fell away from him, and his bones cracked as they reshaped themselves into wings and long sharp feet. Blood pooled from his mouth as his skull crumbled, making way for a beak.

A magpie that used to be Elder Fisher shook itself free and went to join its brethren above the Alder, a caw escaping its newly formed throat.

Oh, he's so beautiful now, Hetty thought. *I wonder if I will look like that.*

Agnes opened the cage and together, Hetty and Kurban stepped out. Agnes cut the rope on Hetty's ankles, and Hetty sighed as the blood rushed back to them.

The Alder reached out, his limbs extending to wrap around the waists of the two teenagers. His branches were warm and Hetty found herself running her hands over them lovingly, a smile pulling her aching cheeks further.

Sacrifice is an honor, children. May your lives feed the hill and those who live on it.

The branches began to squeeze tighter, lifting Hetty and

Kurban towards the Alder. Hetty laughed at herself. How could she have thought the Alder didn't have a face? His mouth was opening now—a maw of jagged stone and sharp glass, larger than she thought possible for his frame.

Slowly, the Alder lowered his branches to his mouth.

And his grove, Alder's Grove, rejoiced at the screams and howls of pain, danced in the red life that spilled over them.

Alder's Grove rejoiced.

Their ailments crumbled.

HAND THAT FEEDS

By Julie Sevens

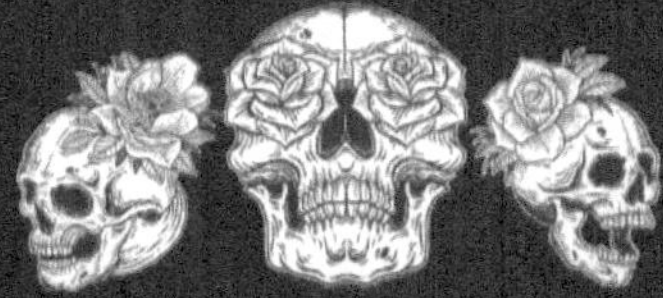

Walt settled into his evening routine—Dinty Moore stew steaming on the TV tray, glass of Pepsi dribbling sweat on a coaster on the sideboard next to his corduroy recliner, reruns of his favorite police procedural on the wood-paneled television. Over the years, the hot bowl had worn a ring in the wood of the TV tray to match the sag in the recliner where he sat.

As Walt put the spoon to his lips to cool his first bite of stew, he heard a scratching noise on his front porch. Maybe a raccoon hiding from the storm, he thought. But the scratching grew louder, more frantic, and this time it was on the door.

Out the window, Walt saw only rain beating on his boxy, blue-striped pick-up out front, rain pouring from a clogged spot in his gutters, rain bouncing off the old wooden steps to the porch. He flicked on the moth-encrusted porchlight. There was a flash of hair, then feet.

With one hand hiding his rifle behind the wall, he threw open the door. "Hey!" he yelled into the rain.

Walt felt the prickle of eyes on him from the woods. He flicked the light back off, let his eyes adjust.

"Didn't you see the 'no trespassers' sign?" he yelled. He

scanned the underbrush, then stepped out, rifle in hand but not raised, at least not yet. "Nothing here worth stealing!"

A chuckling noise came from his right, around the corner of the house. He spun toward it.

Now what in the Sam Hill was that? he muttered to himself.

He listened for movement; heard only rain. His ears always had stuck out a little, and despite all the jokes about elephants, his hearing had never been perfect. Lately, it was getting worse. Duller.

The flash of hair and pale sprinted by again, in front of him this time. Walt's hand clenched the shotgun, but before he could lift it, he froze.

The trespasser couldn't have been more than eight or nine years old. His matted hair hung muddy in his eyes. The boy stopped at the edge of the stubbly, rocky grass, not quite behind the shed. Walt slowly hung the rifle back inside and put his hands out, trying to calm him.

A flash of lightning lit up the sky and the boy darted again, hiding under the overhang of the shed.

"Now, it's alright, boy." Walt said. "I'm real sorry to startle you. You were just trying to get outta the storm, then?"

The boy nodded. The rain was soaking into his clothes, a black leather bomber jacket two sizes too big with no shirt underneath and a pair of jean shorts. His feet were bare and had to be cold in the pools of rain forming in the mud.

"Come on up here, then," Walt said. "We'll sit here 'til it stops."

The boy sprinted to the porch, quick as the lightning cracking in the sky above. He hesitated at the steps, but a sudden gust of rain chased him up. Dirty brown water ran in a rivulet from the short, thick hairs along the back of his neck down into the jacket. His toenails and fingernails were long, jagged, hadn't been cut in too long. He smiled a crooked smile; something sideways about it.

"You live around here? I didn't think anybody did, but then I guess I only own these twenty acres and it's a whole world out there."

Walt followed the boy's gaze inside, to the TV tray where steam rose from the bowl of stew.

"Would it be alright with your folks if I gave you a snack?"

The boy licked his lips and patted the door, his ragged fingernails scraping a flake of old, white paint off the storm door. The boy's feet seeped wet mud into the carpet when Walt opened the door for him.

The kid stared at the wall above the TV. Walt's wife, Martha, had called it 'Walt's Wall of Tchotchkes'—badges from the fishing derby, a shelf with their son's 40-year-old baseball trophies lined up, the framed first invoice his local short-haul trucking company had sent out. The kid was focused on a singing Big Mouth Billy Bass.

Walt pressed the button, and the fish came to life. The boy chuckled, a strangely pitched laugh that lasted too long. Below the fish, Walt had hung a photo of him and his son from the same trip to Florida they'd bought the fish on. In the picture, his son wore a white polo with yellow and blue stripes across the chest, one Walt remembered him wearing often. Walt winced at the thought of his son, wondered when they'd last talked—the calls had fallen to a trickle once Martha was gone.

The boy stopped laughing as suddenly as he'd started and ran into the kitchen. Walt followed him and found him on the floor in front of the sink.

"Come sit over here, kid." He cleared a stack of old mail from Martha's place at the table, wiped a layer of dust from the seat. Once the kid sat down, Walt started opening cabinets, trying to remember what kids liked to eat. He brought back a pack of saltine crackers and a jar of apple butter.

The boy shoved three crackers in his mouth, vertically, squares disappearing into his mouth. He coughed on the dry crumbs, so Walt got him a can of Coke. The boy slurped at it, smiling. Then he shoved his hand in the jar of apple butter and licked the thick layer of it off his fingers.

He patted Walt's arm, too slow and too hard, then scraped his chair back and walked out of the kitchen, back over his muddy footprints on the carpet. The storm door whooshed open.

"Hold on a minute, where's your mama?" Walt asked. "Will you get home alright?"

By the time he got to the door, the boy was gone, the only sign of him the muddy footprints he'd left behind.

Walt wondered if the forest was the only thing parenting this boy.

On Tuesdays, Walt drove his truck down the pitted dirt road to the paved street at the edge of the forest. Tuesdays were grocery trip days, and Walt would fill up the bed of his truck with bags from the IGA in town. This week, Walt decided to add a few things to the bottom of his list. After 'coffee (instant)', he'd added snack cakes, mac and cheese, apples and chicken nuggets.

Walt whistled as he searched the shelves for the blue box of mac and cheese.

"Well, Lizzie, how's it going?" Walt asked the woman reading the ingredients on the side of a cereal box.

"Hey, Walt. How's it going out there? You doing good?"

"Can't complain. You? How's Alice?"

Lizzie looked up from the box. "We're good. Might go on one of those river cruises in Europe this summer."

Walt let her words hang in the air before he said, "Lizzie, what would happen to a kid that lived in the woods? No folks, just them?"

"I guess they'd send someone to pick them up, take 'em

down to the county seat. Find some foster parents. Something happen?"

"Nothing to worry about I don't think. Maybe just a kid who wandered a ways from home. If I need to, I'll call the sheriff."

"Make sure you do, it's cold out there nights." Lizzie's eyebrows didn't settle back down until Walt had turned his wobble-wheeled cart into the next aisle.

He checked off the last item on his list, still thinking about the worry in Lizzie's eyes.

On his walk back to his truck, Walt put two quarters in the newspaper machine and pulled the door open with a creak. The front page was all about a vigil for a missing man from the town over, some truck driver who spent his free time on his Harley and volunteered to take the children's hospital's long-term patients on rides.

Nothing about any kids run away, like he'd half-expected.

A wisp of the memory of his old beagle, Jumper, rode in the car with him on the way home. Jumper had come out of those same woods behind the house, freshly missing the tip of one ear, years ago. Walt had slowly made friends with him, first leaving kibble out by the shed, then the porch, and eventually Jumper had joined him in the recliner every evening and slept at the foot of his bed.

Never did like to be outside alone, though. Not once he'd gotten used to Walt.

Walt turned on his Tuesday police procedural as the sky darkened, but he hesitated in front of the microwave. He paced the kitchen holding the can opener, then left the stew can on the counter and sat down in his recliner without supper. If the boy came back, he'd show him some table manners. See if he could get a word out of him.

Walt lowered the volume on the TV and perked up his ears, listening for that *scratch-scratch-scratch*. In the last ad break, just as Walt's stomach was starting to rumble and he was going to have to eat without his guest in order to take his pills, he heard the floorboards on the porch creak.

Outside, the boy was standing on an old milk crate looking in Walt's window. He clattered to the floor when Walt opened the door, then scrambled to stand up straight.

"You coulda knocked, scout," Walt said, rapping his knuckles on the scratched wood door.

The boy turned and whistled at the woods, his breath ballooning fog from his mouth in the cold.

A red streak of hair flashed behind the shed, then disappeared. The boy whistled again, a more insistent sound, and the red hair poked around the corner.

"There's two of you?" Walt slapped his knee.

The little girl stepped out from behind the shed, dashing to her brother's side. She was a full foot shorter than him, old enough to have lost the baby fat but not by much, her sharp chin poking out like a newly grown-in tooth. Other than the red hair, she looked just like the boy.

She wore an adult-sized black t-shirt as a dress, a strip of rag tied at her waist as a belt. The arms hung to her wrists. Her legs were encased in mud. The boy had changed clothes, was now wearing a new-looking white polo with blue and yellow stripes on the chest. Walt's eyes caught on the pattern of stripes.

"What happened to your coat you had?" And where'd you get the shirt?

They flew past him into the kitchen, the boy sitting in Martha's spot again, the girl leaping up to crouch on the table, dirt flaking from her knees. She looked at the chair Walt pulled out for her, darted her eyes at Walt, then back to the chair.

Lead by example, he could hear Martha saying.

He turned the stove burner on under the pot of water, and the electric smell of burning dust rising from the stove tanged the air. The kids sat stone still, waiting. Walt tried to imagine his son sitting that still at the dinner table and couldn't picture it.

He handed them each an apple as a reward for waiting patiently. The girl's teeth, each one as sharp as the next, sank into the flesh of the apple. The apple was soon polka-dotted with serrated bites torn at random from the surface. Her teeth and the way she ate reminded Walt of an alligator.

"Slow down now, nobody's gonna take it from you," Walt reassured her.

The oven timer dinged, and Walt put two plates of mac and cheese in front of them, then sat down with his stew. He was the model of polite eating—elbows off the table, napkin on his lap, all the rules his own grandma taught him. The boy and his sister scarfed their food, slurped on their apples, stole from each other's plates.

Later, as he was cleaning up, the sharp edge of the Dinty Moore can sliced his thumb. He pressed it hard between his other thumb and forefinger, sucking in a cuss word. The blood seeped out despite the pressure and dripped warm down to his wrist.

The girl grabbed his arm in her hand, her fingers pressing into his flesh.

"Oh, I'm alright, don't worry. I'll find a band-aid around here somewhere."

She pulled his hand to her face and sniffed the rivulet of blood. Walt pulled back on his arm, but the girl's tiny hand overpowered him with surprising ease. He managed to drag her toward the sink and get his hand under a running tap, hoping she'd let go.

The sharp point of her tongue darted out and sampled his wet skin.

Walt jumped back. Anger pumped his heart faster. The

little girl was looking up at him with her big, doll-like eyes, retracting as she sensed his anger. He took a deep breath and resolved to call the sheriff in the morning; he was sure now that nobody was looking after them but him.

They were gone again, as soon as they licked their plates clean, another thing Walt wanted to work on. This time he caught a glimpse of them through the woods, headed straight east. He'd look on the map and see what might be out there.

He rubbed his throbbing thumb. The skin around the cut had begun to itch, and Walt shivered under the porch light.

Wednesday, Walt had a doctor's appointment in town. But when he went out to start the truck, the starter wouldn't turn over. He spent hours tinkering with it, but nothing could get it purring again. His hand still itched something fierce, and it had started to turn red around the cut, but the doctor wouldn't do anything over the phone.

Finally, he slammed the hood and gave up. He'd have to get a mechanic to come to him, and ever since Bill had retired, he couldn't find a good mechanic who would do that.

On his way to the mailbox—way out on the road, he normally drove to it—Walt decided this was just one of those days. Buzzards circled overhead, signaling that—on top of the truck dying and his injured hand—he had something dead to clean up in the yard.

As he walked up closer, Walt gasped. He'd expected a raccoon, a possum or a deer, but heaped in the scrub on the side of his dusty driveway was a pile of entrails, bones, and fur. Must have come from a dozen different animals.

What kind of predator made a cache like this? They hadn't had a mountain lion or a bear in decades. The flies buzzed in the pile, and it stank even in the cold. Walt set back toward the shed to get the red can of gasoline he kept. He'd have to burn it.

The acrid gas smell barely covered up the sweet stench of decay when Walt poured it on the heap. He pulled a bandana up over his face, but it still stung the back of his throat. Some of the kills were fresh, blood still drying on the wounds. Others were old, bloated fur matted in rot. They all burned, though, fat crisping in the heat.

He retreated to his house, watching the black smoke rise from the putrid heap through the kitchen window.

He picked up the phone. It rang in his ear until Grace, the sheriff's dispatcher, answered.

"Let me talk to Sheriff John, would ya?" Walt said.

"I can pass him a message. He's out right now. Or would you talk to the deputy?"

"Tell him it's Walt Hollenback."

Grace cleared her throat in response.

"Grace, you know I take care of myself out here. But I got a real problem out here, not a knocked-over mailbox like the townies call for. You got any missing kids you're looking for?"

Muffled noises shuffled in his ear, then John picked up the line.

"Whatsa matter, Walt? You alright out there? What's this about missing kids?"

"Listen, John, maybe you can help me out. I got a couple of kids out in the woods here, and I don't think they've got anyone looking after them. Seems like they're sleeping rough, and nobody's feeding them but me the past two days. Lizzie Pasternack told me maybe we should get them to the courthouse and get them some help."

"A couple of kids?"

"Yeah, a boy and I think it's his sister. They don't talk much."

The muffled noises returned in the background.

"Walt, does the girl have red hair?"

"Yeah. How'd you—? There's another thing. I think I got some kind of predator out here too, so I'm worried the kids might come across it and get hurt. So maybe sooner than later on getting them out of there."

"You said you've been feeding them?"

"The boy came on Monday during the storm. Last night, he brought the girl back round suppertime. I expect they'll come back tonight; they're real hungry."

"Okay, Walt, listen. I want you to call me when you see them again. I'll wait down at the farmhouse. If they see me in your driveway, it might scare 'em off, but you make sure you call the second they get there. Don't give 'em a chance to skedaddle."

"See you then."

Outside, the column of thick, black smoke was tapering off.

That evening, it was a little warmer, and Walt sat on the porch with a glass of lemonade. He set the cordless phone next to him and pushed the rocker back with his toes. The mud was scrubbed out of the carpet, the kitchen table was clean and dusted, and the radio was playing a low tune to keep him company.

He'd turned the oven on, so it'd be ready to make chicken nuggets for his guests when they arrived—he needed to keep them here long enough to follow through on the sheriff's plan. The lemonade was slippery in his hand, the glass covered in sweat mixed with condensation.

The sun set, long shadows spreading into one another until they covered everything. The boy had arrived about now the day before, but there was no sign of him. Maybe he did have someone looking after him.

A groundhog lumbered by, skimming through the unmown grass near the trees. It froze near the shed, nose twitching, tiny front paws in the air. Then it took off back the way it had come, fur jiggling as it ran, and dove under the side of the porch.

The daylight in the woods had faded to a deep, gray blur. Walt thought he saw a flash of red hair, but no one emerged from the woods.

Night fell, a photograph developing in reverse. Beyond the slices of light from his windows, the darkness circled Walt and his cabin. He heard rustling in the brush, a twig snapping.

"I got the oven on for you, if you're hungry," Walt called out.

The rustling stopped. Then, a long whistle—the same the boy used—rang from the dark. It was answered by a second, several yards to the left.

He tried for an encouraging tone. "No need to be shy, come on then!"

Walt could just made out the silhouette of the boy and his sister next to the big maple tree at the edge of the yard.

Then another silhouette next to them.

"How many of you are there? I probably got enough. Come on out of the woods." Walt put his drink down and touched the back of the phone.

A high-pitched squeal of laughter was the boy's response. Then, he whistled again.

This time, he was answered by a chorus of whistles and trills.

Walt stood up and took an indecisive sidestep toward the door. He glanced at the gun rack just visible through the crack in the door, then looked at the phone again.

The shadow of the boy and girl moved closer, and Walt saw the glint of their eyes, shining yellow-green. They blinked, slow, in unison.

Walt took another step toward the door.

A dozen more pairs of eyes gleamed at him, twinkling like fireflies. They blinked too, the slow flicker of their eyes moving through the trees from one to the next.

He reached for the handle.

The forest came alive, the woods suddenly echoing with feet scrabbling across the dry leaves, roots and stones. They moved together, like a flock of birds turning and twisting in the air, and they dove at Walt as one.

SUMMER LAMENT

By Keily Blair

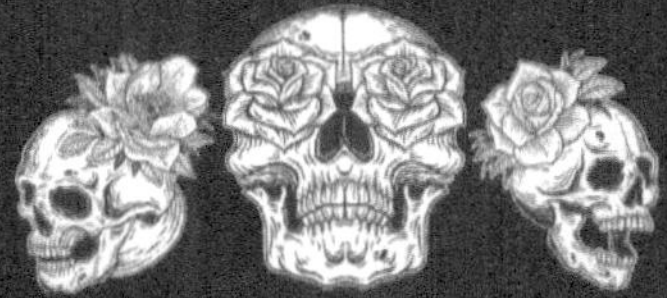

I didn't remember much about my hometown. Every so often, I smelled sweet cut grass in June's golden hair, tasted rich honey on her lips. Her hands brushed against me with light, feathery touches, like leaves rustling in the wind. When she sang, it was with the power of church wedding bells echoing over fields of dancing wheat, and the beauty of birdsong high above my head, out of reach. Summer stretched on forever in her blue eyes, past orchards of apples, stalks of corn rising tall above the earth.

If you looked close enough, something waited for you at the end of infinity. Its name danced on your tongue, and you didn't know whether to laugh or sob or slice your own throat open to stop it from coming.

You had to close your eyes, then. I always did.

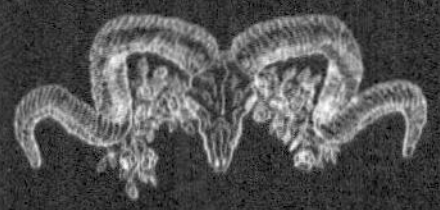

The summer crops grew in chaotic, wilted rows when June Harper graced Crescent Lake with her reviving presence. The few animal sacrifices made for the year's harvest hadn't gone over well, and famine would set in if we didn't act. June's arrival brought a wave of relief to the small town, along with a cascading fear of what would happen should we fail. Most held the general belief June had been born to save us, quell the evil choking the life out of our crops and children. She drove through the town in a shiny new car, drawing envious eyes wherever she went. Most people believed she would stop by her mother's first, pay her respects.

Instead, she came to see me.

I wiped the sweat from my brow before two hands, ice cold from the air conditioning she blasted in her shiny car, reached over my eyes, blinding me.

"Guess who?"

My heart pounded, beating like the hoofs of a horse against the hard, red clay at our feet. My tongue swiped at my dry lips, a futile attempt to moisten the cracked surface.

"May," I said.

Her hands released me, and I turned to see her arms fold over her chest.

"That stopped being funny in second grade, Holly," she said.

"June," I said.

She froze at the way I said her name, a light blush dusting her cheeks. Or maybe it was me, hoping it wasn't just a light sunburn coloring her face when her eyes met mine.

For a moment, things were weird. A solid ten years stretched between us, murky like the lake water stretching out for miles around our birthplace. June's golden hair shimmered like a discovered treasure, tied behind her in a loose ponytail. Her manicured, sky blue nails left crescents in her tanned arms. Every exposed inch of bronzed skin beyond her tank top and denim shorts remained flawless, as though she hadn't traveled to the part of the map where 'there be dragons'.

My breath caught as I sized her up. She'd grown an inch or two, but not much since high school. I'd shot up like a weed in tenth grade, the year after she left. Dryness lingered in my mouth as I avoided thoughts of my hands on her thick thighs, my lips pressed to hers.

"You're staring, Holly," she said.

Her tone was light, teasing, but there was a note of hesitation she'd never held before.

"What brings you back to town?" I asked.

"It's a small town," she said. "Surely you've heard."

"Your mother."

"Good riddance."

I kneeled to inspect a wilted stalk of corn, and June crouched beside me. Her breath tickled my face, sweet with a hint of strawberries. She reached out to touch the stalk before I could stop her, frowning.

"Crops don't seem to be doing well this year," she said.

I bit my tongue, swallowing the tale of a swarm of locusts devouring our harvest last year, and disease the year before. My excitement upon seeing her faded by the minute, replaced with a white-hot anger blazing through every vein, the unfairness of everything charring my insides.

"Come on," I said. "I'll take you to see your brother. He's missed you, you know."

The lie came easily, and she seemed to believe it. We stood facing each other. I handed her my truck's keys, and she walked to it, humming an old hymn she likely didn't understand the meaning of, even now.

I glanced down at the wilted stalk of corn, but it was now green, upright, revived by June's touch.

By the time we reached her mother's home, her younger brother was the only one there. June entered the house after giving Dwight a quick hug. While she wandered through the musty living room and down the hall to the bathroom, Dwight embraced me, clapping me on the back.

"May the Shepherd gaze fondly on you," he said.

"And herd you to greener pastures," I said.

He pulled away, expression grave.

"You do this town a great service, Priestess."

The corner of my mouth almost twitched into a smile. Would it be different if their mother hadn't told Dwight about June's role in the upcoming ritual? He turned away from me, and my teeth clacked together hard as I tried to turn my attention away from such thoughts.

June reentered the room, gazing up at the large image of a lamb. A shepherd stood in the distance, patient as the lamb ran from him. The shepherd had no face, but something about his lack of a profile made the painting so much more sinister, as though the figure holding the crook knew he didn't have to run to catch his stray lamb.

"Do you mind giving us a moment, Dwight?" June asked.

Her gaze remained on the painting. A rush of ice water flooded my veins.

"Of course," Dwight said.

He shot me an apologetic look, but I ignored him, focusing on June. The front screen door banged into the house, and we were alone among piles of patchwork blankets and musty floral furniture. June threw her arms around me, inhaling.

"Stay with me?" she asked.

Before I could reply, the earth shook.

Fine China—or perhaps what her mother passed off as 'fine'—fell in the display cabinet, crashing and shattering. The faux chandelier, made of plastic and little glass, swung as June swayed into me. I planted my feet on the ground, steady, used to having the world sway beneath me in recent years. We were long overdue on delivering the lamb.

June looked up at me. Or I thought she had. Her eyes

rolled back in her head, leaving the whites exposed with blood vessels bulging. In the reflection of the moist surfaces, shadows writhed behind me, but when I turned nothing was there. The earth's fits ceased, everything becoming still, a stagnant pond with a glassy surface.

"Funny," June said, her eyes returned to their normal amber, "I don't remember earthquakes hitting Crescent Lake."

She laughed, but something hovered on the edge of her mirth, a heavy cicada song dizzying my mind. My eyes narrowed as she turned from me, and I thought of doing it then, perhaps with a poker from the fire. The taste of iron filled my mouth at the thought of all the precious blood soaking into the carpet instead of the thirsty, cracked ground. What sort of doom would wait for us after? What sort of scorched earth and infinite madness would rise from below to claim its lost, sweet blood?

June didn't know her own power. Didn't know how, long ago, it seeped into my pores and possessed me.

With a coy smile, June raced up the stairs, taking two at a time. I followed, hands jammed in my pockets, keeping them to myself when I entered her childhood room. It stood untouched, a shrine. My gaze landed on the fluffy pink comforter, an assortment of ten decorative pillows on her childhood bed, marks of her mother's rapidly declining sanity. A single bookcase pressed against a wall, stuffed with knick-knacks and an empty terrarium once home to a turtle we found while roaming the shore along the lake.

I tried not to look at the art lining the walls, the strange beauty of the sketches to be found there. They lined the walls like wallpaper, rustling in a warm breeze I kept trying to tell myself wasn't there.

She explored the room, glancing at me as though asking for permission. I'd been told she'd do this. It was simply part of the ritual. The lamb explored its old pastures. They didn't tell me I'd be in her shadow, heart breaking every time she picked up one of the many gifts I'd given her over the years.

June didn't look me in the eye. All confidence evaporated. Her hand shook as she lifted her old sketchbook. If she noticed the meaning behind the drawings, she said nothing. She didn't even notice when I moved to stand behind her until I spun her around, lips pressing to hers in a feverish kiss.

Her tank top landed on her desk lamp. My belt buckle struck the floor. I forgot the Shepherd and his borrowed lamb, the feel of the ritual knife heavy in my hand. Instead, I drowned in the release of years of built-up adolescent frustration and love for something I could never keep. June moaned and gasped beneath me, and my heart searched for a god willing to let her stay.

We made love until our bodies could no longer handle the heat and fatigue gripped us. June slept curled next to me, mumbling ancient horrors in voices not her own, in dreams she'd never remember, cities of ruin and fire, rivers of blood and plague. My skin burned from her touch, seared as though I'd laid out in the sun for hours. I stared out her window at the night sky, praying to every deity from every religion created by man, hoping for some absolution.

I received no answer.

When I woke June the next morning, her eyes snapped open, revealing black voids lacking even a single star. They swallowed the light as she stared up at me, smiling. Her fingers brushed my face, leaving the warmth of the sun behind them. She blinked, and her eyes were golden honey. I moved to sit at the edge of the bed, gathering my clothes and dressing with her eyes boring holes through me.

"I'm going to the gas station," I said.

She sat up, clutching my arm. The will of a god was strong. The elders warned me about this a month before her arrival, years after they had placed my father's ritual knife in my hand and named me 'Priestess'. I'd thought the years we spent apart would be enough to resist her, but perhaps the madness running through her veins seeped into me somewhere along the way.

I reassured her, told her I would be back. Her grip slackened, and I all but ran out of the room, heart thundering in my chest, blood roaring in my ears. When I made my way down the stairs, Dwight was nowhere to be seen. A frown appeared on my face as I stepped outside the house. Maybe he'd left us alone, knowing our history couldn't be resolved in the presence of onlookers.

The walk to the gas station drew plenty of stares from people on sidewalks, people who crossed the street to avoid me like there was already blood on my hands. The ground shook below, and several frightened shrieks rose into the air. I kept walking, hands shoved in my pockets, at ease on the shuddering earth. Murmurs filled my mind, voices speaking in unknown tongues. The Shepherd would wake soon.

My dad told me about the ancient god long ago, right around the time he introduced me to the barn the town worshiped in. The Shepherd was a creature of ruin and madness, of despair and disease. I'd always wondered why June never showed up when she came of age to enter the barn for weekly worship, for the honor of sacrificing the fattest calves and lambs.

My fists clenched, and the ground stilled. I hurried into the gas station, jumping ahead of a woman walking up to the counter from the back of the store. If she glared at the back of my head, I didn't care. Most folks in Crescent Lake preferred gossip over confrontation. When the attendant looked at me, I picked out the cheapest unfiltered cigarettes they had.

"Thought you quit smoking after your daddy died," the woman behind me said.

I turned to her, clutching the pack like a lifeline. Mrs. Grant, a town elder, stared at me with a mixture of disdain and fear, her lips pressed into a thin line. Her gaze swept over me, lingering on the red burns along my arms.

"You've been busy," she said.

"I don't have time for this," I said.

Before I could leave, her hand caught my shoulder.

"She's a lamb, child. Same as the others we've given to Him. Try not to make this harder on yourself."

I wrenched from her grip and left the gas station. The sun beat down on me as I walked further and further, continuing on until I could no longer make out the faces of the people in town staring after me. I brought a cigarette to my lips, lit it, inhaled. Tears pricked the corners of my eyes.

I imagined June lying across the altar, her trusting eyes watching me with the closest thing to love she was capable of feeling. How many cuts would it take for her to stop looking at me with those beautiful eyes, reassuring me even as The Shepherd's blood left her body and returned to the monster below us?

To speak of such things was blasphemy.

Something moved in the field to my right. I crushed the cigarette beneath my boot and made my way through the rustling rows. A few months before, crows tore apart each of the scarecrows, one by one. Their frenzy lasted hours, but the warning couldn't be clearer. That night, I felt the Shepherd's touch on my mind, felt his words slither into my brain, and I repeated them at service as though they were holy scripture.

Return what is mine.

My mouth grew dry as I remembered the voice. It had been soft and dry like the wind through corn husks, as solid and hard as the stones at my feet. I reached out to brush aside the stalks, my heart picking up speed.

A scarecrow stood in the middle of the field, swaying in the breeze. His arms stretched outward, and his movement made him appear to wave at me. I snorted back a laugh.

Another laugh rose a short distance away, matching mine in its hysterical notes. My eyes narrowed, brow furrowed. I cupped my hands around my mouth and called out to the voice.

"Dwight?" I asked.

I walked through rows until I burst out of the green maze and into Mae Wallace's garden. The figure lay between a rosebush and a few colorful pansies, a shadow writhing about on the damp, dark soil. Mae stood a few paces away, one hand clasped over her mouth as she stared. At first, my mind couldn't make sense of what I saw. The dirt blended so well with Dwight, who appeared to be shivering with the force of his laughter, rolling around on and coating himself in the black earth.

No, not earth.

Black, shiny ants covered the man from head to toe. He tossed back his head in laughter, striking a decorative stone beneath him, but he remained conscious. Giggles rose from his mouth, dark with insects crawling inside. His eyes opened wide, and the ants regained their ground by crawling on the whites.

Mae, frozen, watched the display. Her whispered prayers reached my ears, her endless begging for the horror to cease. I pushed past her, heading for the green hose at the side of her house. Precious seconds flew by as I struggled with the tangled mess, listening to Dwight's laughter dwindling, ceasing. By the time I returned to him, turned the hose on, and sprayed, he had grown still and quiet.

The soil around Dwight turned red orange as the ants melted away, returning to their former state as red Georgia clay. I swallowed hard, dropping the hose, which spouted cool water onto the thirsty, dry grass at the foot of the dead man. Mae's shriek pierced the air, but my own ears rang as the world swam at my feet. My knees struck the ground first before the rest of me followed, my face planting into the soil. The Shepherd's voice filled me, and my body arched with the pain of his jagged words cutting through me.

Return what is mine.

Only when the last word slithered across my tongue did I realize I'd spoken the words aloud. I retched into the grass, heaving even as my empty stomach protested. The taste of iron lingered on my tongue, and when I spat into the grass, blood tinged my saliva from where I'd bitten my tongue.

He'd grown impatient.

Mae rushed over to help me stand, but I waved her away, wiping the spit from my lips and the dirt from my face.

"What did the Shepherd say?" she asked. "You whispered something."

"Nothing new," I said. "Take care of Dwight, will you? Call up Hugh or Jack."

Mae offered to drive me back to June's, not even concerned when I told her where I'd spent the night. I thanked her, but left without another word. I looked back only once to find her standing over Dwight's body, hands clenched into fists at her side, lips moving as though in prayer.

June sat on her mother's floral couch when I returned, dread leaden in the pit of my stomach. Her head slumped to her chest, lips moving to form words of some language lost in the passage of time. I examined the dining room table, the plate of untouched, cooling pancakes in the center. A bit of flour dusted June's nose.

The Shepherd's words lingered in my mind, nasty old cobwebs, clinging to me when I tried to brush them aside. I thought of Dwight, laughing as the ants stung him, pumped him full of venom. My stomach churned again at the image of his swollen body.

I walked over to June, leaning closer to hear the words rumored to drive my great-grandfather to madness. Perhaps a touch of insanity would help steel my resolve.

June grabbed the front of my shirt, yanking me to her level with surprising strength. Her eyes opened, pupils dilated.

"I want to go home, Holly," she said.

"You are home," I said.

She bared her teeth in a snarl. Her hand slapped me across the face, whipping my head to the side with the force.

"I want to be with Father," she said.

June released me, and I tumbled into her lap. Her hands clapped over her mouth, tears welling in her eyes.

"Your face," she said. "I don't know what's gotten into me. I'm so sorry."

As if I could ever be mad at her. Sweet June, who used to sell flowers from her mom's garden to earn the money to buy us ice cream each summer. She'd taught me to read when teachers lost patience with me, when they had treated dyslexia as some curse from the gods. June, who'd been my first kiss when she caught me crying the night my father revealed my fate to me.

I pulled her close, inhaling the scent of wildflowers as though they had been woven through her hair moments before. Nothing in this town belonged to anyone. The priest or priestess chose marriages. Food stores dwindled or overflowed at the will of the Shepherd. Men died from swarms of ants, or rather dirt turned into insects and washed away by a simple garden hose.

My arms tightened around June. No. This was mine to keep.

Outside, the sky darkened. A moment later, a streak of lightning split the sky, and thunder roared overhead. The first drops of rain fell, striking the house as the wind howled through the trees. June's shoulders shook with the force of her sobs, tears soaking into my shirt.

June tried her best to make a simple dinner I'd recognize from our younger years—black-eyed peas, cornbread, collard greens. I joked she was trying too hard, and she rolled her eyes, swatting me with a spatula she'd yanked out of one of her mom's kitchen drawers. We sat down, and though customary prayer, grace, rose in my throat like bile, I swallowed the words and unfolded my hands, reaching for the butter.

We sat in what I assumed to be comfortable silence before I noticed her staring at me, despondent. She'd barely touched the food. Instead, she'd moved the items around on her plate, pretending.

"Something wrong?" I asked.

"When do they want you to do it?" she asked.

"Do what?"

She sucked in a deep breath.

"It's okay, Holly," she said. "I've seen it, you know. The altar. White roses. The tears falling from your eyes with each stroke of the blade on my skin."

Mist clouded her eyes, but I couldn't speak. My hand remained frozen around my fork, my throat dry from the last bite of cornbread.

"Mama always said my father would come back one day," she said. "That he missed me."

I slammed my fist on the table to break whatever hold her spidery thoughts had on her.

"I'm not going to do it," I said. "They can't make me. We're leaving."

Her gaze met mine, her eyes wide. She shook her head.

"You can't," she said. "You can't just abandon this town. The Shepherd needs his blood returned to him. I need to go home."

"We can leave," I said. "Nothing has ever mattered more than you, June."

"The town—"

"This place is a cancer, rotting more with each generation daring to sacrifice another daughter, another innocent."

I rose from my seat, and she mirrored the movement. As I made my way around the table to her, I had the sinking fear she would run before I could reach her. She didn't. Instead, she turned to meet me, wrapping her arms around me.

"There's nothing for me here but you," she said. "Nothing has ever mattered more."

We moved like twin tornadoes, whirling through the house, packing anything and everything we might need to start a life outside of town. I insisted on the more practical stuff—a good pocketknife, matches, canned food, first aid kit. She wanted to bring a beloved, worn journal and her mother's only fine necklace—the one with the emerald butterfly. When I snapped at her sentimentality, she revealed the location of the safe, opened it. Not much remained—a few hundred dollars, papers we didn't need, and her mother's wedding ring from her marriage to Dwight's daddy. I stuffed my wallet with cash, and June put the rest in a duffel bag she swung over one shoulder. The edge of the journal poked out the top of the bag, and a sigh rolled out of me.

They were waiting for us at the bottom of the steps, right next to an open suitcase. Harry and Freddy West, twins I'd shared my first beer with during the time I'd tried drowning my feelings for June. Harry, his gentle eyes hardened with resolve. Freddy, his famous grin swept away by his monstrous scowl.

Between them stood Mrs. Grant, whose eyes softened only a fraction upon taking us in.

"You know she can't stay," she said.

A gun rested at Freddy's hip. His fingers rested on it. Harry's arms folded across his chest, showing off thick muscle. I swallowed hard. If I fought, they would hurt me, maybe even kill me, to take her away. It left me with few options.

"Take her," I said, raising my hands.

"Holly?" she asked, reaching for my shirt.

I stepped out of reach, taking the steps down slow and smooth as warm molasses. June dropped her bag and ran. My eyes closed as the twins ran past me, as her screams for help filled the upstairs hallway. Mrs. Grant stepped forward, put a hand on my arm.

"You're making the right decision," she said. "The only decision."

Harry carried June down the stairs, though she kicked and hit and clawed at every inch she could reach of him. Her reddened eyes met mine, her feeling of betrayal showing like scum on the surface of a murky pond. Mrs. Grant nodded to me, my hands still raised. Something cold and hard pressed to my back, and the odor of Freddy's breath—beer, cigarettes— drifted up to my nose, which wrinkled in disgust.

"I'm sorry, dear," Mrs. Grant said. "You're the only one who can perform the ritual."

"Let her keep her bag," I said. "It's harmless. We'll burn it with the rest of her."

My eyes caught June's. Black tears oozed from her eyes, though her face was devoid of any makeup. Mrs. Grant startled at seeing the strange sight, and the gun shook against my back. A scream tore loose from June's lips, a banshee's cry, breaking windows and leaving my ears ringing. She growled, spouting words in a tongue meant for none of us. Blood trickled out of Mrs. Grant's ear as she motioned for Harry to do something, but he appeared too stunned to understand her.

I understood the feeling. My hands fell to my sides, and the world spun around me, my ears ringing as though June's body had triggered some inner alarm with her shriek.

I knew what I had to do.

"We all have obligations, June," I said. "You didn't really believe we were running away, right? You know it's part of the ritual. Take care of the lamb. Let her believe she is loved."

June bared her teeth in a hateful snarl, her eyes endless blue voids in her skull.

"We're all pawns," I said. "Be grateful I bothered to know you at all. I can't promise the bleeding will be painless, but you'll be long dead before the burning."

June spewed more words in the vile, wrong language none of us knew. The more she spoke in her cursed tongue, the less I wanted to be awake. Pain spiked in my head, and something warm spilled from one of my own ears.

Freddy lay on the ground behind me, eyes closed, the gun gripped in his hand. I dove for the suitcase, digging around until I found the earplugs I'd packed earlier to help with my insomnia. Stuffing them into my ears, I whirled around in time to see Harry had dropped to his knees, and Freddy held his gun to his own head. The gun went off against his temple, a loud bang followed by utter silence.

Blood pooled beneath what remained of Freddy's head.

I scrambled for the gun as Mrs. Grant reached into her purse. The last inch of the barrel of her small revolver made it out of the bag before I fired at her chest. She stumbled back, blood blossoming on her ballerina-pink sweater, spreading and spreading. When she collapsed, only Harry remained.

June lay on the ground, Harry nowhere to be seen.

"Get up," I said. "No time to pack the car."

Her blue eyes gazed up at me, the endless voids of summer. They caught me for mere seconds before I looked away, but I wasn't sure what damage would linger.

"Don't touch me," she said.

"June," I said, "your brothers and sisters before you never displayed this kind of power. We've never delayed a ritual this long. I don't know what will happen if we stay here."

She said nothing, stubborn as a mule as always. I kneeled next to her, still clutching the gun in one hand in case Harry returned with more townsfolk.

"You know I didn't mean it," I said. "If you honestly don't know, then at least think of this: I'm you're one way out of this town. You can't make it without me."

June didn't look at me as she rose, plucking her duffel bag off the floor. We hurried out to Dwight's truck first, and I prayed to any god listening for the car to be fueled. Whether it was dumb luck or one of the gods answered, the tank was full.

I drove us around the lake, following the path June had into town. The further we drove, the more things changed. Rows of corn wilted as we passed. The moon took on an eerie pink, then red, glow. My hands gripped the steering wheel tighter, and I chanced a look at June in the passenger seat. The gun had been between us, but it rested in her hands.

"June?" I asked.

"If we leave, this town is dead," she said.

The earth shook beneath us, growing in intensity with each half-mile we put behind us. I reached for her hand, and though she hesitated, she covered mine with her own.

"I've made the right decision," I said. "A town built on blood isn't worth saving."

We drove onward as the earth shook. In the distance, flames danced in the town. The lake spilled onto the shore in heavy waves.

Then it was gone.

I stopped the truck, gazing at the endless expanse of desert all around us. I'd never stepped foot in such a place before, had never seen the sand and shrubs stretching on as far as the eye could see. After a moment of silence, I backed the truck up, trying to find the mysterious border between the town and desert, but nothing appeared.

Maybe we destroyed the town. Maybe it existed on some plane separate from the one we found ourselves on. We never agreed on any one idea.

June squeezed my hand, and together, we drove across the desert toward a beacon of light in the distance, what we hoped was a haven.

EAST MARION

By Ryan Marie Ketterer

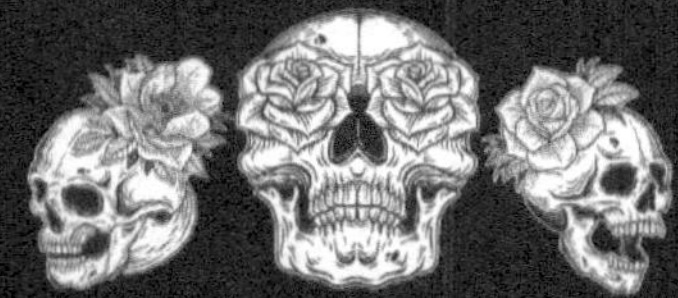

East Marion was, despite its name, in the western part of the state. It was snuggled alongside I-47, an interstate highway used by travelers just passing through on their way somewhere more interesting. In fact, I-47 curved perfectly around the small town, rather than slicing straight over homes and businesses like major interstates normally did. Those that drove this part of I-47 noted an eerie stillness settling around them.

It was as if something was trying to slow their progress, as if their cars were forced to drive through dense clouds and thick sludge.

At the very peak of this I-47 curve, there was a single exit—Exit 3 for those familiar with the area. Exit 3 was the only exit that led directly to East Marion, specifically by way of a long, straight road, creatively named Main Street. All other routes to East Marion were winding and inefficient.

A woman who went by the name of Bonnie—whether or not this was her real name does not matter—had taken up temporary encampment outside the East Marion Wawa. The employees of the gas station needed to shoo the wandering woman away before the town's exciting day could begin.

Upon leaving the trash-riddled gas station pavement, Bonnie made her way down Main Street. On this day, the road was particularly busy, with the residents frantically preparing for the East Marion Mother's Day Parade.

T he residents of East Marion were friendly to Bonnie's face, despite her sunken eyes and drooping jowls, keeping their true judgments hidden within.

"Hey there!" Martha Moore said, one hand waving while the other clasped a child's hand.

"Welcome to East Marion!" Cathy Jackson shouted from across the street, pushing a pram.

"Do let us know if you need help finding your way around," Delia Owens said, in a hushed tone. "Don't let the folks here overwhelm you."

Bonnie wasn't able to reply before the woman hurried off, scolding a young boy pretending to have a sword fight on a skateboard.

These were not the only children that Bonnie could see. Kids of all ages bounded around the town center, playing and crying and yelling as kids do. Their similarity in appearance to one another was striking, but Bonnie did not care enough to notice.

The three-story, glass clock tower of the East Marion Credit Union struck noon, and the bell's jingle echoed throughout the small town square. This hypnotic little tune brought about a sense of belonging and hope for every resident of East Marion. For Bonnie though, it simply reminded her that now might be a good time to eat, as her stomach grumbled loud enough that anyone nearby might hear.

Inside the small and quiet East Marion Diner, the drifting woman ate eggs and bacon, scalding her mouth not once, but twice, on the burnt coffee.

"In town for the parade?" t he waitress asked.

Bonnie said no, that she was just passing through, and that she hoped to leave before things got busy. In the far corner of the diner, sitting in a cramped booth outside of Bonnie's line of sight, the only other patron spun a padlock on his finger as he observed the drifter.

While Bonnie scraped the last vestiges of scrambled eggs from a scuffed ceramic dish, the ladies of East Marion bustled outside.

"Those will be lined up along here, behind the barricades." Martha Moore was signaling to some teenagers who held a pop-up tent.

"The cake came out beautiful, didn't it?" Cathy Jackson beamed as she looked at the desserts spread across several tables. "East Marion red and gold!"

"Pass me the tape," Delia Owens said to the skateboarding boy, who now jabbed an invisible enemy, as she held a colorful array of balloons.

Slowly but surely, Main Street in East Marion was transforming. The town already had a strong sense of pride, but every effort was made to ensure that parade day was a most special day.

Not all things were going smoothly though.

Elsewhere, the men argued.

"You must have left the cage open!" Mark Moore was angry, pointing fingers.

"I locked it, same as always!" Charles Jackson attempted to defend himself, but there was an undercurrent of doubt in his voice.

"The cage has never failed me." Ray Owens' confidence was always welcome but plainly useless in this situation.

The danger of the missing parade star presented a true danger to the residents of East Marion, and was thus frightful enough to call in the mayor. When the men first summoned Mayor Samuel Lewis, they were nervous he would be angry with them, but the folks of East Marion needn't have worried about each other's temperaments; even in the most stressful situations, East Marionettes kept their cool.

"While eating lunch, I thought of the perfect idea!" Mayor Samuel's alternative   put the men at ease.

"I'm so glad Mayor Samuel has found us a replacement," Mark Moore said, his tone satisfied.

"It's not like we could have a parade without it."　Charles Jackson smiled at the other two men, feeling accomplished. "I knew Mayor Samuel would come through."

"Time to rig 'em up, I s'pose," Ray Owens said, as he jumped onto one of the floats.

The East Marion Mother's Day parade was a bit different than the parades held in other towns. To start, there were only two floats. Both were identical, simple things: a metal bar jutting up from a sparkling clean, dark-stained wooden floor. The bar stood approximately five feet high, loose ropes hanging from the top.

With a solution to their dilemma, the men carried on, readying for the coming parade.

Back downtown, Main Street was flourishing. The women corralled the children and jockeyed for the best view.

"I can't wait to see the new one," Martha Moore said, her voice vibrating with elation.

"Hard to believe it's been a whole decade."　Cathy Jackson was laughing as she shook a rattling toy in front of her pram. "I still feel the buzz from last time!"

"The years certainly flew by," Delia Owens said, shaking her head at the passage of time.

By now, the crowds had gathered, clogging the sidewalks. Children tried running past the barriers into the closed street before the adults pulled them back.

The distant thunder of drums began, and the jumpy crowd simmered. The brass and woodwinds soon followed, as the East Marion High School song became audible. The crowd began to chant.

Go East Marion Cougars!

The high school band emerged on Main Street and the crowd went wild. Behind them, the color guard spun and contorted, all while holding massive flags with the town's emblem.

With the crowd in a proper frenzy, it was showtime.

Mayor Samuel Lewis stopped the floats from moving into view.

"Welcome, everyone, to the Ninth Decennial East Marion Mother's Day parade! Today marks the ninetieth year our small and resilient town has said NO!"

The crowd erupted.

"Ninety years since we said NO to the medical risks associated with childbirth!"

More cheers.

"Ninety years since we said NO to destroying the bodies of the beautiful women in our community: our wives, the children, and the women who raised us!"

The crowd danced and celebrated with passion.

"Today we all come together not only to celebrate what we've accomplished here in East Marion, but also to retire Mother Eight and usher in a new generation, a new decade. I can't wait for you all to see Mother Nine."

Mayor Samuel fed off the crowd's fervor.

The first float moved into view and paused before the raucous townspeople.

Mother Eight hung from the once loose ropes tied to the float's metal bar. Her thin wrists were knotted above her head and her limp body hung all the way down to the beautiful, stained float floor, her pale white skin exposed in the bright spring sun. The men had done a great job cleaning Mother Eight. Her hair was shaved—head, armpits, and vulva alike— and her oily skin glistened.

"Mother Eight gave East Marion nine new children, nine wonderful children! To retire Mother Eight, we ask Ike Owens, Mother Eight's first product, birthed for this community, to please join me on the float."

The trouble-making, skateboarding boy next to Delia Owens ran forward and jumped onto the float next to Mayor Samuel.

The mayor handed the boy a knife and said, "You

remember what I told you, right?"

Ike Owens first nodded and then stabbed. Over and over, the boy stabbed. Blood leaked down Mother Eight's clean, convulsing body. It splattered onto Ike's shirt, onto his Vans, onto his skateboard. He smiled the whole time,   even as he carved apart the breasts his mouth had never known.

Mayor Samuel waved the second float forward as the East Marion High School band continued to play. A gray tarp covered Mother Nine.

Go East Marion Cougars!

"Who wants to meet Mother Nine?" Mayor Samuel grinned and looked around, pointing to the dancing kids and the jumping adults. He knew how to work a crowd.

He ripped the tarp away from the float to reveal a writhing beauty. She was hung low enough that she was able to sit directly on the float floor, her bare skin only safe from splinters thanks to how well the men had stained and cleaned the wood.

The arms and legs of Mother Nine were spread wide and secured with more rope. Between her legs was a beautiful bouquet of spring flowers, blues and purples, a perfect Mother's Day medley. A pink primrose flower adorned each nipple and a collection of orange poppies sprouted from Nine's mouth.

Mayor Samuel pulled a rope attached to Mother Nine's arm, simulating a waving motion. "Say hello, everyone!"

Oohs and aahs, rippled through the crowd. The kids waved their hands passionately in return. The men nodded their heads approvingly, patting each other on the backs. The women showed no signs of jealousy, but instead commented on her eye color, her height, her figure—speculating, of course, what type of children she would bear for East Marion.

Bonnie's eyes flitted back and forth in horror at the crowd's excitement. She was unable to respond though, not just because of the lovely spring flowers gagging her, but also because her tongue had been cut out.

And with that, Mother Nine's decade began.

THE HOLLOW KING'S BRIDE

By Wynne F. Winters

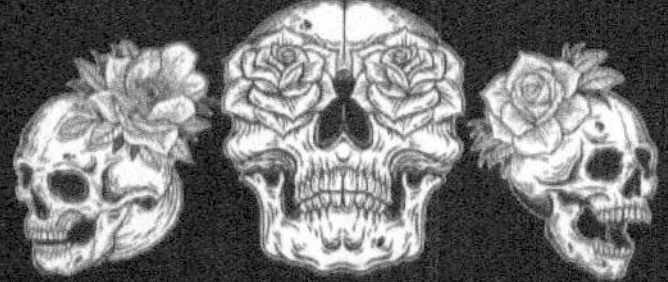

Imogen Grace stood before the mirror and thought she'd never looked less like herself. Her chestnut hair, usually worn in a simple braid, was elaborately piled atop her head, the veil's comb nestled just so. Her humble, homespun dress was replaced by a trailing white gown with a profusion of lace at her wrists and throat.

Her mother, Mairead, knelt at her feet, plying a few last-minute stitches in the hem. Her grandmother, Eabha, finished her updo, pinning a few stray hairs into place. When all was done, they stepped back to see the result, mother on her left and grandmother on her right.

Imogen looked beautiful. And terrified.

"Just breathe," her mother said, emerald eyes holding her daughter's. "Be brave, sweetheart."

Her grandmother, stooped with age, clapped a hand on her shoulder and raised her chin defiantly, the curve of her jaw echoed in her granddaughter's face.

"Be bold, love," she said, giving Imogen's shoulder a squeeze. "Be ruthless."

With that, the three Grace women set off into the warm summer night.

All the town gathered in the village square, from the oldest pensioner to the littlest babe. They were bound to witness—this night was for their benefit, after all. A ritual conducted every thirteen years to ensure prosperity. For a thousand years, the fields had grown golden with wheat, the orchards ripe with fruit, and the cows fat with milk, as long as the townsfolk provided an offering to their agrarian deity.

As the newest family in town, the Graces were obliged to bear the burden: a bride for the Hollow King.

The town square was an old space, the central fountain worn over years of exposure. Every shop and household was shuttered, the lights extinguished. Torches lined the streets, cast flickering light along the cobblestones as Imogen, flanked by her mother and grandmother, approached in her wedding finery.

Three men awaited the young bride. The first, a well-dressed, portly man who served as the town's mayor, held a flower crown, which he gingerly placed on Imogen's head, careful not to disturb her veil. The second, a somber man clad in a vicar's garb, sprinkled holy water from a metal flask, murmuring a blessing. The third man was dressed simply, his expression obscured by a bushy beard. As the head of the blacksmith's guild, he presented a golden ring to the crowd, wrought in the shape of intertwining branches. Hundreds of eyes watched the firelight glint along the delicate workmanship. Instead of giving the ring to Imogen, he held it out to her mother, who received it with a solemn nod.

Appropriately attired, Imogen turned to the north, where her future husband waited.

The walk was a long one. Three fresh-faced virgin girls carried her train, careful to keep it above the dusty cobbles. In accord with tradition, Imogen held a bouquet, the flowers gathered by the local widows—yellow chrysanthemums for prosperity, longevity, and wealth; magenta orchids for love, thoughtfulness, and charm; and pure-white lilies for innocence.

Her knuckles were pale where she gripped the stems, but her face was unreadable.

The crowds watched her pass, the remaining Grace women a few steps behind, and the three men after. When the wedding party reached the town's edge, the townspeople began to follow, filing into a large queue. No one pushed or shoved, though children darted here and there, too young to recognize the evening's import.

The path passed the fields where crops grew plentiful. For such a large group, it was strangely silent, the only sounds the shuffle of feet and a soft, gentle rain as the townsfolk tossed handfuls of rice, leaving a trail in their wake.

The road grew narrower as it entered the woods.

The trees, thick with summer leaves, blocked out the stars, rendering torches the only source of light.

The crowd marched, unnaturally quiet. Eventually, an orange glow appeared in the distance, growing larger and more imposing with every step. At last, the path gave way to an expansive clearing with an enormous bonfire burning vigorously in the center. Before the bonfire stood two figures—the wizened old apothecary and her pimple-faced apprentice.

At the other end of the meadow, beyond reach of the firelight, lay two stone doors set in the ground. No one dared look their way, even during the long wait as the procession came to a stop.

When all were finally assembled, the wedding party stepped away, leaving Imogen before the apothecary. The stooped old woman blinked her rheumy eyes, then glanced at the townsfolk.

"We are gathered here today," she said, her reedy voice carrying through the stillness, "to join this bride to her husband in holy matrimony."

Imogen trembled as the old crone spoke.

"Do you," the apothecary said, holding Imogen's eyes, "take the Hollow King to be your husband?"

Imogen involuntarily glanced at her mother and grandmother. Her mother's clasped hands were white knuckled, her gaze filled with fear. In contrast, her grandmother's eyes were clear and calm. When she saw her granddaughter looking, she merely nodded.

Taking a deep breath, Imogen squared her shoulders. "I do."

The old apothecary nodded to her apprentice, who shuffled over to Imogen's mother. Mairead Grace looked like she didn't want to oblige, but her own mother squeezed her shoulder. With a trembling hand, Mairead offered the ring in an open palm.

The apprentice plucked it from her without a word and shuffled back to the apothecary, holding it out in one grubby hand.

The apothecary took it with great ceremony, then extended her hand to Imogen. "Give me your hand," she said, not unkindly.

Imogen fought the urge to wipe her palm against her wedding dress and placed her slender fingers in the apothecary's grip. The wizened old woman searched her eyes and hesitated for just a moment, the golden band glinting in the firelight. Then she slid the ring home, where it fit perfectly.

"I now pronounce you husband and wife!" she proclaimed.

The crowd all bowed their heads, as if they were at a wake and not a wedding. Six men stepped forward, clad in black, and surrounded Imogen. All were strapping; Imogen seemed even more fragile in their midst. None looked at her as they marched around the fire and toward the darkened end of the clearing, as if Imogen were a prisoner and not a newlywed bride.

Even set in the ground, the stone doors managed to loom. Three massive wooden bars lay across their face, and a pair of chains made an 'X' over, links locked to four iron stakes sunk deep in the ground.

The six men unlocked the chains, hauling them away

before moving the bars. When the doors were free, they grasped hold of the iron rungs, sweating and straining. It took all six to move the stones, which fell to earth with a thunderous crash, revealing a black pit. One of the men fetched a torch from the bonfire, giving it to Imogen with a look of pity. By its flickering light, Imogen saw a series of worn steps carved into the earth itself, disappearing into darkness.

Terror gripped her heart so hard she could barely draw breath. In a moment of weakness, she looked back.

Her mother and grandmother stood at the edge of the firelight, hands clasped. Mairead raised an arm as if to wave, then thought better of it. Eabha merely watched, jaw set.

Imogen nodded to them, wishing for one last chance to say goodbye. But the town was waiting. With a shudder, Imogen turned back to the stairs and gathered her skirts, then started down.

The earth was moist as a womb. The passage twisted downward, so close in some places that clods of dark soil clung to Imogen's dress. Gnarled roots hung from the ceiling and grasped at her hair, nearly dislodging her veil. The torch trembled in her hand, casting phantoms in the dark nooks pockmarking the staircase.

She'd descended a good way when a distant *boom* shook the passage, sending loose dirt raining down. For a moment, she thought it was a thunderclap or earthquake, but a second soon followed, nearly sending her tumbling. It was the stone doors, she realized. She was sealed in.

Knowing there was no way back wound Imogen's fear tighter, like a spring on the edge of breaking. It was suddenly hard to breathe in the dank space and she gasped great lungfuls of air, thinking of the poor souls who woke to find themselves buried alive.

This is my grave, she thought, and bit her lip against the blind panic threatening to overwhelm her.

How long she stayed like that, she couldn't say. But at last, her breathing slowed and her grip on the torch tightened. Below, her husband waited, but he would not be patient forever.

Eventually, the stairs came to an end. Imogen found herself at the entrance to a vast cavern. Intricate pillars, cracked and tumbled in some places, rose three times a man's height around the space. Along the walls flaked the remains of a painting—hounds on a hunt, it seemed. Shattered tiles covered the ground, roots prying apart what little remained. Holes in the ceiling let through shafts of moonlight, casting the space in eerie illumination.

And there, standing at a raised dais at the cavern's center, was the Hollow King.

Even at this distance, Imogen could see he was tall—taller than any man—and thin, with stick-like fingers. As he approached, she realized his skin was rough and bark-like, his matted hair like tangled vines. Shiny black eyes peered through the mess as he loomed over her. This close, she was nearly overwhelmed by his stench—the smell of leaves molding; of small, furry bodies decaying; of mushrooms covering damp, worm-filled earth. It took the last of Imogen's strength to keep from vomiting.

He grasped her with hands as strong as iron. Frightened, she gave a little cry and dropped the torch, leaving it to smoke and sputter on the chipped flagstone. The Hollow King cradled her to his chest where she held her breath, trying not to inhale the terrible odor. She still grasped the bouquet, and as her new husband carried her over the broken cavern floor, she held the blossoms to her nose, trying to remain calm.

A large beam of moonlight spread over the dais, illuminating a marble altar. Once, the stone may have been white, but it was dark with centuries of stains. The Hollow King's steps crunched as they neared. Peering over his enormous hands, Imogen saw the white, shattered shapes of bone.

The Hollow King laid her tenderly upon the altar, brushing her hair with moldering fingers as she trembled, the whites of her eyes showing. She clasped the bouquet to her chest as if clinging to a lifeline.

The Hollow King loomed, casting her in shadow. As she watched, he opened his mouth—wider and wider—unhinging until it filled her vision, the jagged teeth gray and mangled, his breath reeking of old blood.

Then he bit into her.

Imogen screamed as the broken teeth punctured her skin, tearing her insides as the Hollow King clamped down. When he rose, he took a piece of her with him, bloody entrails hanging from his jaws as he thoughtfully chewed.

Imogen couldn't breathe. Her vision went white with pain.

This was death. This was what death felt like. She coughed, blood staining her chin as she watched her newlywed husband consume her flesh.

He turned back to her, gore staining his lips as he opened his mouth to take another bite. But then he retched, tree-like body twitching, and pulled away, his great shoulders shaking as he bent and spilled the contents of his stomach beside the altar. Imogen watched, a look of disgust on her face. With enormous effort, she pushed herself into a sitting position.

"Bit off more than you can chew?" she asked, her voice tight with pain.

The Hollow King turned his beady eyes on her, then retched again, the vomit black and stinking of iron.

Slowly, Imogen rose, silver moonlight setting her gore-splattered dress aglow. Blood dribbled from her mouth and poured from her stomach, but she didn't seem to notice now. When she spoke again, her voice echoed, as though three spoke instead of one.

"Our blood is too rich for the likes of you. It contains the magic of ages."

The moonlight grew sharper, spilling like water over her wounds. Where it touched, the flesh mended, leaving it whole and hale, as though no teeth had ever marred it.

The Hollow King vomited, his legs collapsing, sending him to all fours. He looked up at her, his chest coated with his own sick, black chunks caught in his jagged teeth.

She stood before him, face passive, and thrust her hand into his chest.

The monarch spasmed, helpless as her fist clenched around his heart. Black sap oozed from the wound and spilled from his unblinking eyes.

"You are my lawfully wedded husband," Imogen said, in a chorus. "Our marriage consummated before the very moon Herself. What's yours is mine, and I claim it now."

With one swift motion, she ripped his heart from his chest.

The Hollow King swayed for a moment, the hole in his chest gushing noisome black ichor. His eyes rolled up and his jaw sagged. A moment later, he collapsed into a pile of rotting sticks and moss, the vines of his hair shriveling into dry husks.

Imogen watched it all without a sound, the heavy heart steaming in her hand. Then, with a singular determination, she bit into the muscle and began to eat.

Bitter sap flooded her mouth, acrid on her tongue, but she forced herself to continue, the heart crunching like autumn leaves beneath her teeth. As she swallowed, a dark tide began to rise within her, whispering the secrets of deep earth, bleached bone, and writhing worms. At her feet, the body of the Hollow King rotted, mildew spreading into every nook and cranny until the corpse disintegrated, nothing more than grave dirt.

The silver moonlight swelled, and from its beams stepped two women: Mairead Grace, her smile full of a mother's gentle patience, and Eabha Grace, her stern face lined with a crone's wisdom. The three stood over the remains of the Hollow King, then turned their eyes skyward, crowns of pearly fire appearing in their hair. They opened their mouths simultaneously and spoke with a single voice.

"We claim our throne."

The cavern began to shake, the ceiling cracking. Moonlight poured in, illuminating the ruined chamber. The altar split and something rose beneath it—an immense throne of bone, skulls adorning the armrests and back.

"This forest is ours."

Roots thickened along the cavern walls, visibly bending toward the freshly birthed throne. Snaking vines swallowed the ruined columns and fragrant summer grass grew over the tiled floor.

The three turned as one, as if they could see the bonfire from here, the line of villagers breaking as the trees around them twisted and stretched, roots turning to gnarled feet and branches to lethal claws.

As one, they smiled, a feral thing full of teeth.

"Now begins our reign. And it shall overflow with tears and blood."

FEED THE NEED

By S.O. Green

Jess found the first bloody flower petal in the hall, right under the coatrack. She dropped her jacket and followed the trail through the house as she found another and another and another. She could hear Blossom sobbing in the bathroom.

"Babe? You okay?"

Past framed photos of them—at the beach, at that sushi place in the city, at Jess's graduation—where they smiled and blew kisses and Blossom's hair was the fire to Jess's coal. In every single one, the flower crown, with its dark, bruise-colored blooms, ubiquitous. A constant reminder of the past Blossom could never forget or outrun or even talk about, and Jess would never dig because love was knowing when to leave things buried.

The bathroom door wasn't locked—lucky, since Jess had been fixing to kick it down—and she found Blossom sitting in the empty bathtub, arms curled around her knees. Blood streaked the porcelain and the wetwall and stained every towel. It soaked Blossom's t-shirt and track pants, because today she'd been feeling strong enough to go out, maybe to the store or just for a walk, and *this*—whatever the fuck this was—had ruined everything.

She longed for this morning, when her biggest problem had been the worry that Blossom wasn't getting out enough, and that the guys at work wouldn't shut up about the damn flowers when they went to the company dinner on Saturday, if they even went.

Jess said nothing. She dropped to her knees and wrapped her arms tight around Blossom's shoulders, and her girlfriend sobbed into her uniform.

"I'm wilting," she whispered, once she could talk. "Jess, it hurts. It hurts so much…"

She broke off into a keening wail, like a wounded animal. Jess squeezed her so hard she thought one of them might break. But they were both stronger than that, and they'd proved it, over and over again. All she could do was hold on until her girl came back to herself.

Once she'd settled, she ditched her company shirt and slacks, cranked the shower on, and held Blossom under the steaming water. It swirled pink around their feet. Petals clogged the drain. Bald patches, seeping wounds, showed where the crown had started to die.

"What the fuck do we do?" Jess begged.

Blossom gulped hard, but she schooled her voice firm and strong, like they'd practiced. "I need to go home."

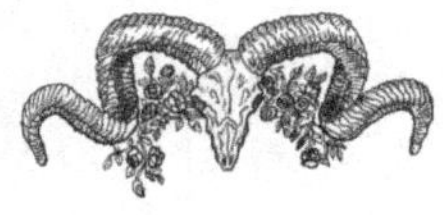

"Blossom, do you know who I am?"

"The Bandorai?"

"That's right. I take care of the Need Tree. And do you know what these are?"

"Antlers?"

"Close. They're branches. The Tree gave them to me, to show that I'm special. Just like it gave you all those pretty flowers. You're special too. We both are."

"I don't think I want to be special. It made my mom and dad cry."

"It's okay to cry sometimes, Blossom. People cry for all kinds of reasons. But you're going to be brave, aren't you? And you're going to come with me like a good girl."

"Why?"

"We're going to do something very important together. We're going to feed the Tree."

It seemed like a fool's errand. From the little Blossom told her on the drive, there was no way to fix it. No one with the 'blessing' had ever lived long enough to wilt, and that had been by design. Anyone chosen by the capital-T Tree—Jess had really struggled with that concept, but she'd grown up in a world of cement and fiber optics, college and causality, rational and orderly, faith optional—belonged to it. Belonged to the earth and to nature and the cycle of all things.

Human sacrifices. That was what it boiled down to in Jess's brain, and it made her mad as Hell. Someone had tried to take her girl away before they'd even met. Fuck going back there.

Only Blossom was dying. Her skin had turned grey and started to dry. The flower petals wouldn't stop falling out, taking pieces of her as they went. If Blossom had needed a kidney or a lung, she'd have given it up without thinking. But she needed to go back to that place, and that?

That made her nervous.

"Maybe drugs would help," Jess said, as she swung their car off the winding forest road into the gas station.

"How?"

"I don't know. Maybe this is like cancer. Dangerous

but survivable. Maybe they could treat it with radiation or something. Or... They could try some kind of souped-up plant food."

Blossom laughed. Dry and scratchy, but the humor was there. She checked herself in the mirror in the sunshade. A fat drop of blood ran down her forehead. Only the tears beading in her eyes betrayed the pain.

"I'll go and clean up. Mind grabbing something to eat after you fill up?"

"Sure. Any requests?"

Blossom rubbed her stomach ruefully. "No more candy bars."

"My sister in Christ, *you* bought the candy bars."

"Yeah, well... That's what you get for letting me buy the food. Do I look like someone who's got their shit together?"

"Soon, babe," Jess said, and squeezed Blossom's knee as tight as she dared. "We'll fix this real soon."

She filled the tank and ducked into the kiosk, walking past a corkboard peppered with missing posters and ancient community notices that looked about twenty years out of date. She scooped up bottled water and soggy sandwiches in bent cardboard. They'd probably have been better off with candy bars.

"Your sister alright?" the clerk asked, as he rang up their meagre lunch. "Looked like she wasn't doing too good."

"She's not my sister," Jess said, "and she's sick. That's why we're taking this trip. She wants to see home, just in case this is her last chance."

Technically true.

"Yeah? Where's home? Not much out this way."

"Need Meadow."

"No shit? Never actually met anyone from Need Meadow before. Way I heard it, no one ever leaves. It's just one, big, inbred hippy backwater. Still, guess they'd need to get new blood in somehow, else they'd have fucked themselves out of existence at this point."

Jess reminded herself that this was the place that had tried to kill her girlfriend, the place that worshipped a carnivorous tree. Would Blossom be upset if she heard this hick fuck talking about her family and neighbors that way?

Or would she think they deserved it, same way Jess did?

"So, we're on the right road?"

The hick laughed as he stuffed her purchases in a plastic carrier. "You're on the right road, sure, but you're heading the wrong way. You should be heading *away* from Need Meadow. No one goes up there anymore. Place is diseased. Groundwater's poisoned, forest's dead all around it. Everyone round these parts knows to stay away."

"Too bad," Jess muttered, and slapped a ten on the counter, "because that's where we're going."

"Blossom, listen to me very carefully. Put on your shoes and your jacket and then come with me, okay?"

"What happened, mom? Are you hurt?"

"Don't worry about that right now. Just do as I said. And be quick."

"Where's daddy?"

"Blossom! I need you to stop *asking questions. Can you do that for me? Please?"*

"Mom, I'm scared."

"Me too, sweetheart. Me too. But it's going to be okay. We're leaving. We're going to go far away and nobody's going to be able to find us."

"Do you think it's connected?" Blossom asked, once Jess had told her the gossip, minus the part about the inbreeding.

"What, the diseased land and your crown? I mean, maybe? Does magic have rules?"

"I think that's probably the point. If it didn't have rules, why bother with the sacrifices?"

"Because people do things for dumb reasons. Like because their parents did them. 'If it was good enough for my folks, it's good enough for me.' Need Meadow ain't so different from every other place in that regard. I mean, shit, I went to college just like mom and dad, and I ended up working in a hardware store. People never stop to ask themselves, 'is this still alright? Is this still something we *need* to do?' They're so worried about what'll happen if they stop, they don't think about what they're losing."

They lapsed into silence as they followed the dense, green tunnel through the sun-dappled wood, scaring blackbirds and shrikes off the rutted country road. Felt like they'd been driving forever, and Jess's bones ached from the ass-kicking the potholes were giving her. Still, it felt better having a physical pain to focus on.

"How you feeling, anyway?" she asked. "We're getting closer. Is it...different?"

"It's better," Blossom insisted. "Less like a brain tumor and more like toothache."

"Wow. Great options. Listen, babe, when we get there, what are we even going to—?"

"Let's just get there, okay? And figure out the rest later."

She put a hand on Jess's shoulder. It took the edge off her anxiety but didn't make it leave. She just couldn't shake the feeling that this was a one-way trip.

They arrived at Need Meadow around dusk. The sun slipped below the forest behind them, turning the sky to fire. Blossom had fallen asleep, cradled by her seatbelt, but Jess had known they were getting close when the trees turned dead and brittle all around and the grass dried out, brown and patchy over the grey earth. A cluster of old, mold-speckled buildings stood on the brow of the hill, and down below, the lake had turned to muddy slurry.

The drive became bumpier on approach and Jess had to stop short of the village proper, in case she fucked the car. Once they were still, she realized what the problem was. The ground all around Need Meadow swelled with thick, black roots, like bloated veins straining under the skin. They reached all the way down to the lake, all the way out into the woods, seeking, grasping, squeezing.

"Well shit..."

"Did we break down?" Blossom croaked, scrubbing her eyes with her bloody sweater sleeves.

"No, babe. We're here. We made it."

Her girlfriend nodded. She hadn't started bleeding again, so maybe that was a good sign. Jess designed to give her a moment, but Blossom popped her door and slid out of the car, obliging her to follow.

"Take it easy," she urged.

"Why? We drove all the way out here to find out if this place could help, and now we're here. I don't want to stay any longer than we have to."

Jess nodded and offered her arm. On the violated ground, she didn't trust Blossom's shaky legs to keep her from falling. They left the road and followed a dusty trail into a grove behind the dilapidated buildings. Jess wondered how the place looked in Blossom's mind, how her memories compared with reality.

Judging by the grim look on her face, not favorably.

"Where are we going?" Jess whispered, because her voice felt too loud in the total silence.

"The Need Tree. I want to see it for myself."

It was the only tree in the grove that still had leaves, even though it was mid-Spring. They were the same dark bruise color as the dying petals on Blossom's crown. Its trunk was a twisted mass of limbs coiling in and around one another until they formed a squat, distended central mass, and the wood was black as coal. Black as the roots stretching out beneath everything.

It was drooping in places, decaying in others, and the whole grove stank of damp rot. If cancer could infect a forest, this was a tumor.

"I take it this isn't what you remember?"

"It used to be confined to the grove before, not spread all around. And it never dropped a single leaf, the whole time I lived here."

She kicked a dried and crinkled pile, which tumbled listlessly apart under her boot.

"So, what changed, do you think?"

"I did," Blossom said, and Jess could hear the hitch in her voice as she teared up. "I caused this, when I left."

"Hey, you didn't leave. Your mom took you, remember? And she probably saved your life."

"And look what happened." She waved at the bleak landscape around them, trending bleaker in the dying light. In the far distance, green treetops reminded them of what had been lost. "It all died, Jess. It's *still* dying."

"So what? Fuck 'em. They brought this on themselves. If it hadn't been you, it would have been someone else. And if it *had* been you, the Tree would have chosen a new victim later. How long would they have had? A year? Two? I mean, how fucking hungry is this thing?"

Something broke a branch with a gunshot crack at the edge of the grove. Jess thumbed the flashlight on her phone and held it high. A guy about their age in a battered, old windbreaker emerged from the gloom, carrying a shovel over his shoulder and dragging a dead possum. He froze in the light, like a deer, which Jess supposed was fair since two stubby, splintered antlers jutted from his forehead, weeping thin trickles of blood into his eyebrows.

"Elan?" Blossom whispered.

"You came back," he breathed. "All this time and you came back. I think I'd just about given up hope."

"Where's everyone else?"

He shrugged. The possum's tail slipped through his fingers, but Jess watched his fingers flexing around the shovel's handle. His eyes flicked from one of them to the other and back, sizing them both up.

"Dead. The Bandorai was first. She thought maybe she could fix the damage by offering herself. Didn't work. It kept calling out. Spreading across the ground. Killed the trees, killed the garden. People started getting sick."

"It chose you, didn't it?" Blossom stared at his broken antlers, hand rising to brush the dying petals on her brow. "To be the new Bandorai."

Elan smiled, but he didn't seem to find it funny. "It's an honor, remember? Especially for me, being a man and all. I've been doing my best. Trying to keep it fed. Nothing works. I guess you only really understand why the old ways were important when you see what happens otherwise."

Jess scoffed. "You were killing people. You were murdering kids. And for what? To protect your little slice of Heaven? For a good harvest? You ask me, you sowed blood, now you're reaping death."

"Those sacrifices did right by us, same as everyone else. Ask Blossom. Before the Tree chose her, it was the happiest time of her life."

"We were children," Blossom said. "We didn't know any better."

"You're right, but knowing better just means knowing this isn't where it stops. You think it gives a fuck about county lines?

Borders? It's going to keep spreading. Shit, have you stopped to listen? Nothing lives here anymore. Every day, I need to go deeper and deeper into the woods."

He waved a hand at the dead rodent at his feet, his scowl deepening. How far had he hiked to find and kill it? How far *would* he have gone if he hadn't found it?

"I used to get lucky. Folks would come out this way looking for a place to get high or get laid. They'd keep the Tree quiet for a month, maybe longer. Then that dried up, once word got out. I managed to get a couple down Roanoke way, or upriver, but I took a bullet when I went back for more. Couldn't even get the slug out. Wound looks like a knothole now. I miss those days, Blossom. I could sleep and not have to hear it scratching around the inside of my skull. Do you have any idea what it feels like to have that *thing* inside your head?"

"Like its roots are digging into your brain and squeezing till you think you'll die," Blossom said, and Elan's features softened, just a little.

"You came back," he said again. "That changes everything."

"How?" Jess demanded, sliding between him and Blossom.

"We can fix this. I know a way. You don't even have to die!"

"Why should we trust you?"

"Well, you ain't got a choice."

The earth moved under her feet. In the heartbeat it took Jess to make sure nothing was reaching for her ankles from the dirt, Elan closed the distance between them. His shovel split her skull with a tinny thunk and she went down like a sawn-through tree, ear ringing and blood running into her eye.

She heard Blossom scream her name before the darkness ate her up.

"What's up? Why are you crying?"

"They tried to pull my flower crown off."

"So what? It's just flowers, right?"

"It...doesn't come off. It just hurts."

"Oh... Well, if someone tries to hurt you, just hurt them back. Make sure they know not to mess with you. Hit them, kick them, bite them if you have to. Gotta do what you need to do. That's what my mom says."

"You don't...think it's weird? Everyone says it's weird that my flowers don't come off."

"Nah, they're pretty. You're pretty."

Elan dragged her back to the cottages and common house of her childhood. By the time they reached his family's old, decrepit cabin, Blossom had bitten him three times, blacked his eye and scraped his shin raw with her boot. When she grabbed the doorframe, he hit her so hard it damn-near knocked her out.

"I'm trying to be gentle," he said, tone pleading. "Don't you get it? I'm going to fix all this. You're gonna be okay."

"You killed her!" Blossom shrieked, and launched herself at him, clawed hands reaching for his eyes.

He kicked her feet out from under her and slammed her on her back. The air blew out of her lungs, then the toe of his boot cracked one of her ribs and she couldn't get it back.

"Ain't the way I wanted to treat the woman who'll bear my child, but..."

"Wha—? What are you talking about?" she groaned, as he hoisted her up in his arms and carried her honeymoon-style into the moldering bedroom.

"Our baby. When we give it to the Need Tree, we'll both

be free. We can leave, finally, and do whatever we want with the rest of our lives."

He kicked aside broken, bloody branches scattered on the floor. The vanity had a hacksaw and a crimson-streaked file resting on it, a clean spot worried in the center of the mirror. How fast did his branches grow? Probably as fast as she bloomed, only he'd never had someone to love them the way she had.

And now she's gone...

"I'll take care of you," he muttered, feverish. "Just nine months. Nine months and then it's over. That's all."

She thrashed as he tried to pin her wrists to the bed and unfasten her jeans at the same time. He slapped her so hard it tore something in her neck. Her bruised brain throbbed. Then he grabbed her by her flowers and the pain blinded her.

She hadn't stopped crying since the grove, since seeing Jess fall. She was still crying now. Sometimes, it felt like all she was good for was crying. Couldn't sleep right. Couldn't leave the house most days. Couldn't give her girlfriend the life she deserved.

If someone tries to hurt you, just hurt them back.

Her hand found his left antler and wrenched. He screamed as the wood split right down to the bone. Blood poured into his eye, over his lips, off the point of his chin and spattered her chest. He tried to push her off and she kicked him where Jess had always told her to kick a man.

He toppled off the bed, grunting and wailing and cradling his junk. She stood up, nearly fell, and steadied herself against the wall. Then she grabbed the bed and flipped it on top of him with an enraged scream.

She blew back through the cabin, tripping over broken furniture, skidding on glass shards and dark stains, then burst out into the night. The moon was fat and full and mournfully bearing witness to the worst day of Blossom's life since the night her mother had come home spattered with her father's blood, bundled her into the commune's old jeep and driven so far and so fast they'd blown the engine up on the interstate.

She thought about running to the car, but her heart lay in the grove, with the body of the woman she loved. She stumbled over the tangled roots of the Need Tree that had reached out across miles to drag her back here. When she fell, they battered her like bruised knuckles through the thin soil. She pushed herself up, but she'd let them beat her to death before she let Elan go through with what he'd planned.

He screamed her name into the darkness. There was only one place she could be going, and he knew it. He'd catch her.

She guessed they'd settle it where it had all started.

The night broke around the Need Tree. It throbbed and shifted and pulsed with light. Her crown was glowing too, and she felt herself drawn closer. The roots beat in the dirt like they were sucking into an immense heart, and in their faint illumination, she saw the skulls and ribcages and hipbones they entangled and toyed with, big and small, smaller and smaller, packed into the earth, buried to feed the Tree. And she saw Jess, slumped beside Elan's shovel. She reached for it, just as Elan stuck his knife in her flank.

"I tried to give you a way out," he said, voice hollow, as she tumbled into a gap between the roots and lay, bleeding into the dirt. "We could have both gotten away. But I guess this is how it has to be. How it should have been in the first place. Maybe, after this, it'll finally let me go."

He groped for the shovel to finish the job, never taking his eyes off her, until his hand closed on nothing, and he realized it had moved. He turned just as Jess brought it down like an axe, right between his eyes.

"You should have finished me off," she growled, as he collapsed.

She jammed the point of the blade against his neck and stamped, hard. His spinal column severed with a crunch.

Blossom called her name. Jess came to her, just like every

other time. She wrapped her arms tight around her, but it didn't warm her the way it should. Cold through and through. She couldn't stop shivering.

"You know what you have to do," Blossom whispered.

Jess shook her head. Her lips moved but only silence came out. She pressed her cheek to Blossom's flowers and something warm that might have been blood or tears dripped onto her forehead like a baptismal.

"You know what I *want* you to do."

How many people had died because of Blossom? Her daddy, her mom, the Bandorai, her friends and family and neighbors, and every person and animal Elan had killed to feed the tree. Almost Jess too. She couldn't have lived with the guilt, but she wasn't going to live, and suddenly she understood what her atonement needed to be.

Elan had been right about one thing. It didn't care about county lines or borders. The Tree needed to be fed. The Tree had chosen.

It had chosen her.

Jess found the apple tree the next day, when she woke up lying on the earth she'd turned the night before. The fruit was off-color and tasted like mud, but it chased away one hollow feeling at least.

The Need Tree looked brighter by day. Healthier. So did the trees standing around it, and the grass had begun to grow back, green instead of brown. She walked back to the cluster of cottages, where she'd buried Elan in an unmarked pit out the back of the big communal building and resisted the urge to spit on him out of respect for Blossom, who'd never had a bad word to say about anyone, even the people who'd tried to kill her.

The roots had slithered back to the confines of the grove. The ground seemed even and alive again, maybe how it had looked when Blossom had been a kid. Given time, the place might even be worth living in.

She'd drive to the gas station and buy food, maybe a candy bar, and see what she could find in terms of tools and seeds. She'd cannibalize the cottages to fix one up, because she only needed a place for one. It'd be hard and it'd only get harder, but it was the only option she had, other than to lie down on that grave and never get up.

The Tree wasn't the only thing that had needed Blossom.

And she didn't know what she was going to do if it ever started to reach out again, but she figured she'd cross that bridge when she came to it. No sense in fretting about the future when you didn't really have one.

She'd know when it happened. She'd hear it.

She checked herself in the mirror in the sunshade, running a finger over the nubs on her forehead, like the beginnings of antlers, just starting to push through the skin. A fat drop of blood ran down her forehead. She wiped it away with a napkin from the glove box.

Looked like she'd come home.

ALTARS IN THE WORLD'S MARROW

By Jonathan Louis Duckworth

Karelia, Russian Empire. 1907.

Sunrise came in a jaundiced blush over the misty peat bogs outside Pudozh. Baron Lydgate, my friend and employer, was still turning in the cot. As I dressed myself, I wondered if I should wake him, but it pleased me to watch him. He had the face of a Byron, a boyish mop of auburn hair and a slender build. Through his nightshirt, I could see the divot in his chest, a little defect in the bone of his sternum that seemed to have been shaped by God to fit my thumb.

I let him sleep and finished dressing. We were here in Russia to hunt reindeer, specifically an albino herd reputed to roam the wilderness beyond Lake Onega. The Salmazero Herd.

Outside our room, in the inn's hallway, Lydgate's Russian cousin was waiting. Count Sikorsky was cleaning his rifle, a German Mauser, while his hulking servant Mischa knelt beside and scraped stubborn mud off his riding boots.

"Mister Cowboy, I trust you slept well?"

The Count's English was as impeccable as his French. He

had his cousin's looks, albeit sharpened, and his gold pince-nez spectacles gave him a severe, owlish bearing.

"Tolerably well, Your Highness."

I tipped my Stetson to him, because I knew he'd appreciate it more than a traditional bow. I'd seen the contents of his saddlebags—the works of Moliere, Hugo and Rimbaud, imbricated with dime store novels about Wyatt Earp and the Little Big Horn. When first we'd met in St-Petersburg, he'd asked me if I'd ever 'scalped a Red Indian'.

"Well, I fear our accommodations in Salmazero shall be rather more roughhewn," the Count said, shoving his cleaning rod through the barrel. "And anyway, you can call me Igor. Out here, we are hunting companions."

"If you say so, Igor."

The Count gave a command and Mischa stopped shining his boots and stood up to full height. I'm not small by any measure, but Mischa—which apparently means 'Mouse' in Russian—had a head on me, easy. He was always smiling, showing off his missing teeth.

Mischa thumped past me and then down the stairs where it sounded like our local guide, a Finn named Jani, was already up and about.

"Is my cousin awake?"

"Not yet."

"I'm not surprised. Percy was always such a languid boy. A queer little thing he was, always fussing with his butterfly collections and reading old books. Tell me, Mister Cowboy, how is it you came to be in his employ?"

I looked to the door, hoping Lydgate would rise any moment now and save me from having to tell the same old lie as I'd told all his friends and relations in England. Always there were questions about the American—the Texan 'cowboy' done up in tweeds and working as game warden on Baron Lydgate's estate in County Kent.

"Well, we met in the Yukon..."

The Count jerked his rifle's bolt to check the breech. "I've heard this story. He was on a hunt, you were a porter on the locomotive, and you saved his life from a moose."

"A grizzly bear."

He flashed a strange smile, framed by his waxed whiskers. "Tell me, what does his lovely wife think of your association?"

"I don't know what you mean."

The door mercifully opened, and Baron Lydgate joined the waking world. He looked and sounded refreshed, recovered from his nightmare. "Cousin! Shall we find the herd today?"

"If God is kind, and if we do not dally any more than we already have," the Count replied.

We set out late in the morning, which scuttled any chance of reaching Salmazero before nightfall. Five men on five horses, following a dirt path through the peat bogs and dark forests toward the furthest edge of Europe. We were all experienced hunters and outdoorsmen, but outside of Jani, none of us had ever been to this part of Karelia. The pines and spruces rising from the peaty soil slanted at odd angles, their tips pointing toward inscrutable mysteries concealed by the milky sky. The ground held enigmas too. Every twenty minutes or so, Lydgate would stop his horse without warning to root around and inspect something.

"We'll never reach Salmazero if you keep fussing over lichens and flowers," the Count said, on the third such instance. "We're in this marshland to hunt big game, cousin, not pick mushrooms and bilberries."

Lydgate seemed not to hear his cousin. "In communing with the soil, we commune with our origins. From the soil we came, and to the soil we return. Man is of nature and yet separate, and we are at once children playing in the garden of Demeter, but also interlopers gamboling perilously at the edge of Pan's sylvan demesne."

On the Count and Mischa's faces was barely concealed frustration.

Jani muttered something.

"What did he just say?" I asked.

"He says there are no birds singing here," the Count said.

I listened. Lydgate also tilted up his ear. Indeed, there was no birdsong, a strange thing for a fair summer day. We resumed our ride, but now I couldn't help but notice that, aside from the steady clop and plop of hooves through the soft, muddy path, a perfect stillness reigned.

A half-hour later, Mischa spotted an old peasant woman wandering the woods about a hundred yards from the path. There were no settlements between Pudozh and Salmazero, but that was only going by our fifty-year-old map.

"Whatever is she doing out there?" Lydgate mused.

"Looks like she's stripping bark from the trees," I said. And as I said that, I saw her take something from the bark and put it in her mouth.

The Count and Mischa exchanged some words in their native tongue and then laughed.

"Mister Cowboy, Mischa doesn't think I could hit her from here," the Count said. "What do you think?"

I turned to the Count, who presently took his rifle from its scabbard on his saddle and shouldered it, and aimed at the old woman. The safety lever was still locked, but it only took a flick of his thumb. The Count's voice sounded jocular, but the look in his eyes behind those glittery spectacles was bare-bone serious.

"What's she done to you?" I asked.

"You haven't answered my question."

Baron Lydgate nosed his horse between us, took hold of the barrel of his cousin's Mauser and pushed it down. "Igor, that's quite enough. Mister Drummond doesn't share your sense of humor. Nor do I."

"Is only peasant, milord," Mischa said. "So many of them. Like herring in ocean, or weevil in grain."

The sun got lower and lower among the trees, first nesting

in the tops of the spruces, then sidling along the trunks, and finally rolling as a golden yolk to the forest floor where it seemed to suspend itself, smoldering like a stubborn coal in a poor man's grate.

We rode into Salmazero under silver-blue twilight. It was more and less than I expected. More, because I'd imagined a little cluster of cabins, not a good-sized village of forty or fifty houses as it turned out to be. Less, because it appeared entirely abandoned.

There were no lights hanging from any of the doors, nor any torches or lanterns in the streets. Many of the houses had broken windowpanes or no glass at all. Some of the roofs had caved in, while others were stripped bare of any thatching and rendered to skeletal timber frames.

"Well, this is a fine welcome," Lydgate said.

My horse was fidgeting under me, tossing his head and tensing his haunches. Looked like the other horses were just as unsettled. It was as quiet as a tomb in the village.

The Count said something in Russian, in a loud, peremptory tone. There was no response.

And then, from behind us, a single word spoken in a girl's voice.

"*Puteshestvenniki?*"

I knew that word; it meant 'travelers'. We all turned our horses to face her. She'd gotten behind us somehow. She was a short, stocky girl, young and pretty in the homespun way of farmers' daughters, attired in a peasant's trappings, hair covered by a gray kerchief. Her blank expression held none of the groveling obsequiousness or apprehension I'd come to expect from the Russian peasantry during my brief time in the country. Her hands and wrists were caked with dark, damp soil.

Mischa answered her in Russian.

From somewhere in the village, a door groaned open and then rattled shut. My head turned in the direction of the sound, and by the time I'd looked back to the girl, there were two more people, blank-faced and dourly attired like her, an old couple. Their hands were also covered in dirt.

The old man said something.

"He says he's the innkeeper here," Lydgate explained, for my benefit. "He says we are welcome to spend the night in their inn."

"Lovely."

The silence now pierced, the shuffle and creak of human bodies began to infiltrate the derelict village, and now faces appeared from doorways and through dusty windows, and little candles lit up to breathe some light into the deepening dusk. They watched us, all these men and women and children in their ragged clothes, their dirty hands, their vacuous eyes.

If any of them ever blinked, it must have been once I stopped looking.

There was no fire burning in the inn's hearth when we entered, accompanied by the innkeeper and his wife and child. I don't think I'd ever seen that before—even the most ramshackle village inn in the middle of summer should have a modest fire going to welcome travelers.

Not trusting the villagers and their dirty hands to bed down the horses in the stables, it fell to Mischa and me. As we led the horses by their reins toward a large, rickety clapboard structure at the edge of the village, the big fellow spat and grumbled something in Russian before turning to me and saying, "There is no smoke here."

He pointed to the stone and clay chimneys and what wasn't rising from their mouths. Cold wind blew in and I couldn't help but shiver. Mischa shivered too.

"Cold night," I said. "And no fires burning."

"*Da*. Very cold for summer."

The stable was, unsurprisingly, in a state of extreme disrepair. The stalls were rotting, the rafters seemed a stiff wind away from collapse, and the ground was bare except for ancient fannings of chaff and old slates of compacted manure. There was the animal smell of any stable, but it was stale, remote, the ghost of a barn's stink.

"What's to stop them from taking the horses while we sleep?" I asked.

In answer, Mischa drew a broad Cossack dagger from the hilt on his bandolier, and then sheathed it again.

We shut the stable door and fastened it shut with a rusted chain.

Back in the inn, Jani and the innkeeper had gotten a fire going with peat and logs, while in the kitchen, the wife and daughter were grinding flour from rye and buckwheat. That there was no food ready might have bothered me, except that for whatever reason, I wasn't hungry.

A full day's ride and I wasn't hungry. Imagine that.

After an hour of waiting, the innkeeper and his wife served us the rudiments of a supper—freshly made black bread, somehow already stale, and a watery soup of bitter roots and stringy, pale meat I couldn't identify. Count Sikorsky didn't touch his soup, and instead opened a glass pot of pickled herring from his provisions and ate them with the bread on a small silver plate, that, per Lydgate, he always carried with him.

While we ate, the family seemed to recede, the innkeeper standing stoically behind the counter while his wife swept the floor with a broom. The daughter hovered around the periphery, dusting windows and wiping the chairs and tables.

At one point, she drifted near the hearth to sweep some ashes into the ashpan, and as she stooped, big Mischa grabbed her by her haunches and pulled her onto his lap.

Lydgate averted his eyes and puffed on his pipe, while the Count smiled wryly as if watching a favorite diversion. If the girl had cried out, I'd have been on Mischa in a blink.

But the girl didn't cry out. She didn't do anything. Her expression was the same blank face as ever. The innkeeper watched with indifference from behind the counter, while the wife couldn't even be bothered to look up from her sweeping. I knew little about the ways of Russian peasants, but this seemed wrong.

Even if she knew not to resist, shouldn't she have shown *something*?

Mischa let go of the girl, and from the disturbed look on his face you'd think it was *his* rump that had gotten played with. The girl, who'd given him no gratification of any kind, had done none of whatever he might have wanted, whether it were supplication or resistance.

After that incident, the family seemed to disappear, leaving us alone in the inn. Lydgate and the Count puffed on their pipes and told stories by the fireplace, Mischa occasionally interjecting. I listened but heard nothing, my mind dwelling on the girl's strange passivity and her family's indifference.

Meanwhile, Jani the Finn kept his vigil by the window, and eventually I came over to see what had engrossed him. Through the window, a gibbous moon illuminated the fields and woods beyond the village. Big, dark shapes wiggled like worms on the turf and mud, and it took a moment for my eyes to reconcile that those shapes were human.

Villagers, a few dozen peasants of all ages, bowing and prostrating and writhing on the dirt under the auspice of the moon.

I slept very little. For as hard and uncomfortable as the cot in Pudozh had been, at least there had not been vermin crawling under the floorboards. Between the scrabbling of hundreds of limbs and Lydgate's snoring, I managed maybe an hour of shuteye. When I woke an hour before dawn, Lydgate's nightshirt was damp against my chest and I felt the tremor in his spine of an ongoing night terror.

I pinched him awake, and he shuddered in my arms and turned his face to me—his lovely, green eyes watery, his mournful, downcurved lip atremble—and told me what he'd dreamt. A hole in the earth, a thread of light, the promise of mystery and revelation, and him crawling on his belly.

"Even now, the vision evanesces, yet I recall an idol of some kind, an altar awaiting in a hollow in the earth of a shape suggestive of such profound truth that I could not turn away."

I smoothed the crease of worry in his brow with my lips.

When we'd dressed ourselves, the others were already waiting downstairs. Because the innkeeper had not returned after disappearing in the night, we were left to our own devices. We ate a light breakfast from our own provisions—salted fish, hardtack and canned meat—and then set out for the first hunt.

The sun rose to reveal a village deserted. As empty as it had been when we'd arrived the night before.

"Church services, perhaps?" Lydgate offered.

"No church in Russia holds services on a Friday morning," the Count replied, then added, with a sneer, "unless it is a Moslem temple."

We followed Jani's lead out into the woods east of the village. It was a warm, pleasant day, and as it hadn't rained the night before, the ground was tolerably firm. The stories about the Salmazero Herd—and they were just that: stories—held that the herd was elusive but never strayed too far from the village it was named after. It didn't take long for Jani to find tracks in the mud—reindeer tracks. That was promising.

More promising was when he found a tuft of snow-white fur snagged on a birch tree's branch. But that was all we ended up seeing of reindeer that day. We spent all morning and afternoon walking through the conifer woods and tramping through dark muck sprinkled with lichens. Here and there, ridges and hillocks offered vistas from which we could scan the horizon, but with so much mist—even late in the day—there wasn't much to scope out.

We were all of us grumpy by the time we stopped in a dry clearing for our midday meal, and the collective mood worsened when the Count discovered his treasured silver plate was missing from his bag.

"The damned peasants," he grumbled. "That perfidious innkeeper, or his daughter. They must have seen me eating off it and coveted it."

I strained to imagine those shapeless people coveting anything.

"Are you certain you didn't misplace it?" Lydgate offered.

"When have you ever known me to misplace anything, cousin? I am not like you; I keep both feet on this earth and my eyes on those around me."

"It'll turn up, I'm sure," I said.

"*Da*," Mischa said, "and then we skin peasant who took it."

Jani, who'd been quiet most of the day, mumbled something to the Count. The Count answered with something sharp.

"He is right, though," Lydgate said. "We have passed many of those holes in these woods."

"Unless the herd is hiding in them, I don't give a damn about any holes in the ground," the Count said.

There was a hole not far from where we were encamped. The moraines of earth around its rim were dark and loose and damp, fresh-looking. A smell arose from it, not the pleasant smell of earth or the sweet scent of peat, but something sour and nauseating.

The Count, in a huff, packed up his things. "Let's continue."

"We haven't even started eating," I said.

"No one eats if I can't."

It was not a sentence that invited argument, not even from Lydgate. Our stomachs growled, but we didn't dare growl or grumble ourselves.

We searched for another few hours. Our hopes were briefly kindled by the discovery of a solitary set of prints—small hooves, a doe or even a calf—but when these terminated at the banks of a forest stream, we all but gave up.

It took us most of an hour to find our way back to the village. It was on this quiet, miserable march that I noticed again the lack of animal sounds. No birds at all. Plenty of freshly dug burrows though. The sun was starting to sink when we came upon a large clearing, one we'd passed on the way out of the village. In that clearing, a young peasant boy was scraping at a birch tree with a knife, much as the old woman had been doing the day before.

As we approached to within two hundred, then a hundred yards, the boy never looked over his shoulder, never paid us the slightest attention. He kept scraping, peeling back strips of papery bark and then removing the harder inner covering to reveal pale wood. From the wood, he took something, a grub, and dropped it into a wicker basket he had with him.

"A most curious sight," Lydgate said.

Beside him, the Count unslung his Mauser, shouldered it, and aimed down the sights. "Game is game," he said.

"Come on, now, Igor," I said. "It wasn't funny the first time and it's not—"

A clap of thunder blew the words from my lips. Cordite stung my nostrils, and the Mauser's sharp report seemed to hang in the air for many seconds, rolling through the forest and resounding off the nearby hillocks. The peasant boy stumbled and turned toward us, for the first time aware of our presence. The startling rose of fresh blood blossomed in his shirt, and he fell onto the forest floor.

Lydgate ran to him first, and Jani and I were close behind. When we reached the boy, he'd already given up the ghost. I felt for a pulse, and his skin felt abnormally clammy. Lydgate was weeping, I felt close to tears myself. I had a kid brother around the same age back in Dallas.

The Count and Mischa took their time strolling over.

"Is there a silver plate in the basket?" the Count asked.

It took every bit of my restraint not to launch myself at him.

The Count peered into the boy's basket, then said something in French and kicked it over. From out of the basket, pale grubs and damp, wriggling worms spilled onto the forest floor.

"Igor, how could you do something so monstrous?"

"Cousin, the Almighty allots every man a peccadillo now and then, does He not?"

"A peccadillo, you say? A peccadillo?"

Gritting my teeth, still crouched over the dead boy, I took hold of my rifle's sling and unslung it, setting it down by my feet.

"We are hundreds of miles from any railroads, any telegraph wires or telephones. This is not England, and you should not pretend it is."

"Murder is murder."

"Is not murder for peasant, milord," Mischa said. And then he laughed. "Like I say, herring in ocean, weevil in—"

Gripping it by the barrel and magazine, I swung my Winchester like a woodsman's axe, and hit Mischa square in his face. The bones in my arms stung and my whole body reverberated as if I'd struck an oak tree. Mischa's nose cracked on impact, and most any other man would have been out like a candle. Not Mischa. He stood there, looming over me, stunned like a brained bovine, mouth hanging open and blood running from his crushed nose.

And then, quick as a whip, he drew his dagger and raked it at my face. I fell on my back just in time, suffering a graze on my cheek. He jumped onto me, pinned me under his knees, and brought the dagger down. I made a cross with my arms and caught his wrists, but his weight and strength pressed the knife down, down, closer to my throat, closer to soft skin and warm blood.

"Mischa!" the Count snapped.

It was remarkable how fast the big bastard climbed off me.

Lydgate knelt by my side. "Linus, are you alright?"

I didn't answer him. Instead, I reached for my Winchester, but before I could lift it, a boot stamped down on the rifle. Jani's pale eyes narrowed; his thin lips made a hard line. It wasn't a threat, more a warning—relent, or they'll kill you.

I wasn't stupid, just a Texan; I knew when to quit, and let go of the rifle.

"Honestly, all the histrionics and pugilism over a worm-eating peasant," the Count said. "I knew my cousin to be a fairy, but I expected better of you, Mister Cowboy."

I had a few choice words for him rattling in my skull, but before I could press them into breath, the corpse of the boy, the boy we'd all watched die, started moving.

At first, it was a twitch of the foot. Not an unheard-of thing for the recently dead. But then the head lolled side to side on the limp neck, and the hands spasmed, and the feet kicked at the dirt, and then the mouth opened wide, and the tongue rolled out.

The boy stopped moving as suddenly as he'd started.

"What on earth?" Lydgate gasped.

Click, clack, click. A sound, like flint striking steel. The boy's throat bulged, and then two long, black wires emerged from his mouth. Six inches of legs and mandibles unspooled from the dead lips, and scampered into the brush, soon lost in the low-lying ferns and bilberry bushes.

In the ensuant silence, Lydgate was the first to speak. "I've heard stories of earwigs in Africa that burrow in men's ears…"

"That wasn't an earwig."

We didn't speak any more of it. Burying the body wasn't difficult. There were so many holes nearby to choose from.

Salmazero was deserted again, but we were all too exhausted to care this time. Inside the inn, deserted as it had been when we left, Jani rebuilt the fire in the hearth, and we ate the rations we'd not eaten earlier in the day. There was no smoking by the fire, no story-swapping. Mischa wouldn't stop glaring at me, and I think I halfway hoped he'd say something and give me pretext, but he kept his sullen silence.

Another unseasonably cold night. As we turned in for the evening, Jani remained downstairs, seated in an armchair by the fire, his Mosin-Nagant rifle laid on his knees. In our cot, I held Lydgate close to me while he wept for the dead boy. He fell asleep first; crying will do that to a man. Me, I hung in like a thorn in the night's side, listening to the creak of old timbers and the hush-hush of wind outside, waiting for the dark to play its hand.

Sometime in the dark, I saw Mischa looming over my bed, the broad blade of his Cossack dagger glinting in the moonlight. I saw him standing there and knew I should do something about it, but my Winchester was so far away, and I couldn't move my arms or legs.

Mischa called me a Fort-Worth-cocksucker and then staked the dagger into my chest.

When I woke up, the first thing I noticed, other than that

I wasn't dead, was the sound in the walls—the scrabbling of vermin again. Only now it wasn't a mystery. Now I knew what the clicks that perforated the tap-tap of tiny claws was.

The next thing I noticed was that Lydgate wasn't in the cot with me. My heart thumped harder and my toes got like ice. The door to the room was unlocked and partway ajar. From the dim wedge of light spilling in, I could see a shadow.

"Sir?"

No answer.

"Percy? Are you out there?"

The shadow moved away, but I heard no footsteps.

Click, clack, click.

I looked up, just as a rat-sized length of armored nightmare dropped from the ceiling and plummeted toward my face. My hand swept out to meet it, knocking the thing out of the air and against the wall. It struck the wall and slid to the floor, its segmented body and many limbs thrashing. Before it could right itself, I rolled out of bed, found one of my heavy boots and hurled it. Bullseye. A sour smell filled the air and the clicking stopped.

Breathe in, breathe out. Steady.

Lydgate was missing, but I couldn't let myself panic, had to steady myself. I dressed quickly, took up my rifle, then hurried down the stairs, hoping against reason that Lydgate might be warming himself by the fire.

Not only was Lydgate not there, but neither was the Finn, and the fire had gone out. More worryingly, the ragged curtains fluttered from a draft blown in from the open front door. The ground was moist outside. The moonlight showed footprints heading out into the dark.

Now hell was well and true on me. I ran up the stairs and thumped the Count's door with the butt of my Winchester.

"Open up, Sikorsky, Lydgate's missing. So is the Finn."

The door cracked open and the Count—with his hair unbrushed, he resembled his better cousin more than ever—

stuck his face out. "What are you blathering about?"

Having no time for decorum, I shouldered the door open, knocking the Count off balance. "I said your cousin's gone and so is Jani."

"Gone? What do you mean gone?"

I told him what I'd seen. That sobered him some.

"Mischa," he said, turning to the bed where the big valet was having a bear's sleep. The Count gave commands in Russian, unheeded. Then the Count tried shaking him, to no avail. I pulled the covers off.

Mischa was on his back, arms at his sides, feet hanging over the edge of the cot. His nose had swollen to twice its size and an unseemly welt had formed on his forehead. He'd died angry, jaw and fists clenched.

"What? What's wrong with him? What happened?"

"Concussion, I imagine. Shouldn't have let him go to sleep."

"You! You did this! You're a—"

I slapped him across the jaw with the offside of my hand. "Focus, man. We've got missing men."

"You just struck me." He rubbed his jaw and stared dumbstruck. "As one strikes a woman."

"Show the other cheek and I'll strike you like a man. Come on, we've got to move."

"What about Mischa?"

I bent over the corpse and pulled the dagger from its sheath and stuffed it under my belt. Could come in handy, I figured. "He's dead. Your cousin might still be alive."

I turned my back on him, and as I did, I heard him grab his Mauser, and heard the bolt turn. "I should shoot you."

I didn't turn around. "And leave yourself alone in the dark?"

I walked out. And after the walls started to whisper and rattle with the motions of hundreds of tiny limbs, the Count hurried down the stairs after me, dressed only in a nightshirt.

We had no lantern, but the moon was bright. It shone on the water welled in Lydgate's footprints. The footprints led out of the village, into the woods to the west of town, the direction of the moon.

"Percy!" the Count called out.

I rapped him on the head. "Quiet. We don't know what we're dealing with here. Best not to make noise."

"How are we to find him then?"

"Follow the footprints."

Up ahead, little puddles of mud and the larger body of a forest pond caught the bountiful glow of the moon. It seemed to me that, against those flashes of silver, dark, erect shapes stood, watching us through the gloom.

"You're no tracker. This is hopeless. Hopeless, I say."

I was figuring what to do, whether to slap him again or just shush him, when the world collapsed under me. One instant, I was on firm ground; the next I was falling, sliding down a chute of loose, damp soil into a burrow.

I reckon I tumbled twenty feet before a tree root caught me between my thighs and taught me a new lesson on what pain could be. I lay in a pile of myself, aching a dozen places, dazed, in darkness, before I got enough of my wits to look up at the shaft of moonlight and see the Count looking down on me.

"Are your injured?" the Count asked. "Can you move your legs?"

I kicked my right leg and experienced a twinge in my tailbone and spine, but when I moved my left, I knew from the leaden weight of it and heat that I'd twisted something. "We had ropes," I said. "Back in the inn, in my saddlebag."

Framed in silver, I could see the twitch of every little calculation in the Count's face muscles. Then his face turned, as if he'd seen something.

"Don't you dare leave me down here."

He didn't answer. His face receded from view.

"Sikorsky!"

I didn't care what else might be down here in this cavern, I bellowed like to break the sky, until my throat and ribs both burned.

I wobbled to my feet. I couldn't find my Winchester, but I still had the Cossack dagger. I felt safer, more whole with it in my hand. But it was a poor substitute for Lydgate's earnest grasp and a full sky over my head.

To my back was a wall of earth and roots. To the other side, an arctic draft spoke to a deeper way into the dark. With no way to scale my way to the surface, I had only one choice.

To press into the underworld.

I left behind the moon and felt my way forward. With each pained footfall, I wondered if it might be my last, if I might slip into a deeper hole, a bottomless yawn, or if something from nightmares might find me. Every so often, I felt drafts indicating other passages, but I kept going straight.

Eventually, I saw light. It was nothing. A thread, a little hair of silver, but I strove toward it. At this part of the tunnel, there was sludgy water that sucked at my boots, and each step was a labor. After what felt like a Sisyphean eternity, I reached that thread of light.

It was a little aperture in the ground, as big as a rabbit hole, at the top of the deep cavern in which I stood, as far from me as the stars themselves.

I almost cried. But there came a sour smell, and the *click-click-click* sound. Not just the click. Footsteps. Human footsteps.

I wheeled around, pointing the dagger. A red glow approached from the vast dark, closing on me. Caught in that glow was a face. A grim, lean face.

"Jani!"

The Finn put a finger to his lips as he drew close. He had his rifle slung over his shoulder and held a torch, the source of the glow, and also of the clicking. It was the simplest of torches, a skewer upon which the burning carcasses of a bundle of dead centipede-things had been wrapped. As the flames burned, their fat rendered and their chitinous plates popped. *Click-click-click.*

Jani took his rifle from his shoulder and offered it to me. We traded weapons, my dagger for his rifle. He couldn't very well shoot a rifle while holding the torch, after all. He motioned for me to follow him, and I had no problem with that.

"What is this place?" I whispered, as if he'd know, as if he could understand me. "What the hell's going on?"

He guided us through winding tunnels that narrowed such that we had to crawl on our knees—that was hell on my ribs and my gamed ankle—and then widened into great, subterranean atriums. In these spaces, the torchlight revealed hideous orchards. There is no other word for what I saw. From the thick chords of ancient roots in the ceiling of the caverns, glistening man-sized pods of fleshy, sallow membranes dangled like fruit. I thought of chrysalises.

I still don't know what was inside of them, but I have a pretty good guess, and if they were chrysalises as they appeared to be, I'd rather not speculate on what their inmates were turning into.

Eventually, mercifully, Jani found us a way into the world, one of the large holes that dotted the forests. We emerged into fresh air and starlight and moonshine. Someone was laughing. It was a cackle, a strained, manic flute of human inanity. We followed that laughter to the foot of a little hillock.

There, with his back to a spruce, his Mauser lying a yard out of reach, was Count Sikorsky. He seemed helpless against the laughter that'd crawled into him. His nightshirt was a tableau of gore and blood, while the pink and gray spools of his viscera even now slid free from their compartment. He smelled like an abattoir, shit and guts and all.

"Hehehe, they're real," he said. "Mister Cowboy, look, the Herd."

He pointed up at the hillock that loomed above us.

We turned just as an animal snorted. It watched us from atop the hill, its antlers and fur—except where stained by the Count's blood—the same color as the moon that hung between its entrail-strewn antlers.

The Count stopped laughing and went silent. The reindeer stag regarded us with an intelligence I'd never credit to any cervine. I knew in that instant why we'd not found the deer; it was the same reason we didn't see any of the villagers during the daytime. They all lived below.

And in that instant, I also knew I had to shoot it. I shouldered the unwieldy Russian rifle, took aim, and pulled the trigger.

Nothing. Because I didn't know where the safety was. I didn't get a chance to look, for in the next blink, the great beast hurtled from its high perch and struck Jani with a crunch.

I ran. Stupid as it was to run, I didn't know what else to do.

Or, I tried to run. I didn't get far before my ankle buckled under me and I fell on my face. I just lay there, shuddering, aching, waiting for antlers and hooves to find my exposed back.

But instead, footsteps crunched through the ground toward me, and a gentle voice spoke. "Linus. Linus, my love, it's all right."

I rolled onto my back. The reindeer, now joined by two others, stood over me, their eyes brooding, their antlers drooped. Between them was Baron Lydgate.

He was dressed in his hunting clothes, uninjured, intact.

"Percy? You're alright. How?"

A breeze ruffled the tousled brown locks on Lydgate's head and his eyes glistened a strange silvery color. "I am better than alright, my love. I am complete now."

Whatever relief I might have felt curdled. "No. Not you."

"There's nothing to be afraid of." He stepped closer, offered a hand.

"Don't touch me. Stay away."

"Let me help you. Let us help you."

"I said stay away." I groped around until I found the Finn's rifle. I turned a little knob on the action—the safety—and sat up to point the rifle square at Lydgate. The reindeer tensed but Lydgate didn't react. On the hillock behind him stood human figures. Peasants, armed with scythes and axes and hammers. "You're not putting one of those things in me."

"Linus, you must listen to me. I—we—will not force anything upon you. But you will be so much more complete once you have a companion. My companion in such short time has expanded my mind to dimensions I never before imagined, offered me glimpses into sublime new vantages and deep truths. It sings to me—O, that you could hear it, the very music of the spheres!"

"I saw what you… What these monsters did to the Count."

"He was unclean. There was nothing one such as him could offer to our body."

"You're talking crazy."

"No, there's nothing mad about it. You see, many aeons ago, before life kindled on this world, there was a great war in the heavens. Two Nameless powers clashed and smote one another from the sky. One fell into the empty oceans, and the Other fell into the earth to mend and recover. It is that Great power to which we belong. A shattered God, you see, but with each body, each cell He joins to Himself, He is steadily rebuilt from us. Until the time that He is ready to rise again into the air and aether, and crown the sun and moon with His magnificence."

I fit my finger into the trigger. "There's got to be a way. If some of you is left, we can escape. We can dig that damn bug out of you—"

"You're not listening. There are such wonders below waiting for you, we have cities in the nighted hollows, glorious altars in the world's marrow."

Behind Lydgate—behind Percy—the villagers were

closing their eyes, while the reindeer shook their heads. They knew I wasn't going to go quietly. Probably Percy did too. But still he tried. There was still so much of him left.

I still pulled the trigger.

Even as close as he was, I missed. The bullet grazed his head and made pulp of his left ear. He stood with his mouth agape. Worse than anything was the devastation and heartbreak carved on his face.

The largest of the reindeer surged at me first.

A Cossack dagger buried into its throat, the stag buckled and collapsed, and there was Jani the Finn, standing between me and the horde.

They had antlers and tools of iron, but as I staggered to my feet and the villagers and reindeer came charging, Jani took a fine plate of silver from his bag and held it toward the moon above. The Count's silver.

The villagers and reindeer stopped. Lydgate, too, snapped to attention.

And then all of them dropped low. The people to their knees, the deer onto their bellies, heads bowed, for Jani held the moon in his hands.

Even now that I had a path to freedom, I hesitated, because the biggest piece of my heart had his nose pressed to the dirt in awe of the figure of the moon. I wanted to grab him, to take him into my arms and carry him across the woods and marshes of Karelia and across the Baltic and all the way back to England.

But clouds were moving in the sky, a gray eyelid sliding shut. I prized my eyes from Lydgate's prostrate form and started shambling away, toward the village.

The horses were gone, of course. Taken, like every other animal or person in Salmazero. Maybe the birds had gotten away. Maybe they, like Jani and I, were the lucky ones.

On foot, with my injured ankle, it took us six days to make it back to Pudozh. I'd never have survived without the canny Finn, who foraged for us and fashioned me a simple crutch. We came to Pudozh with no money and clouded with suspicion. The town's functionaries, including the mayor, had seen us leave with a Russian count and an English baron, only to return with neither. Even if I were in any state to tell the tale—or had the faculty in the local lingo—no one would have believed us.

We only stayed in Pudozh long enough to get my leg treated and to get food in us. Jani stole us a pair of horses and we rode out before the mayor could think to wire the authorities in St. Petersburg. From there, we rode to Finland, where Jani had friends and I could find passage back to America.

But before we left Pudozh, Karelia had one last chill for me.

While a doctor splinted my leg properly, I lay on his bench and looked out his window at the rooftops. It was a cold day, a very cold day for early September. Whiskers of smoke rose from many of the chimneys. But not all of them.

That on its own could be ignored. It was what I saw after leaving the doctor's house that broke me.

In the streets, where children were playing in the mud, a single girlchild stood apart. This girl, with her red kerchief, worried at the bark of one of the little trees lining the street with a pocketknife. Her hands were filthy, caked in dirt. I watched her at her work until a woman, also with dirty hands, came to claim her. When she did, mother and daughter both noticed me, and as they did, their expressions changed. From blankness to a bitter, corrosive anger.

Because they recognized the one who'd spurned their love.

ABOUT THE AUTHORS

PATRICK BARB

Patrick Barb is an author of weird, dark, and horrifying tales, currently living (and trying not to freeze to death) in Saint Paul, Minnesota. He is the author of the novellas Gargantuana's Ghost (Grey Matter Press), Turn (Alien Buddha Press), and The Nut House (serialized in Cosmic Horror Monthly), as well as the novelette Helicopter Parenting in the Age of Drone Warfare (Spooky House Press) and the forthcoming dark fiction collection Pre-Approved for Haunting (Keylight Books / Turner Publishing, October 2023). He is an Active Member of the HWA and a Full Member of the SFWA.

Visit him at patrickbarb.com.

KEILY BLAIR

Keily Blair (they/them) is an autistic, queer writer, as well as Managing Editor of the Signal Mountain Review. They hold a BA in English: Creative Writing from UT Chattanooga, where their nonfiction won the Creative Nonfiction Award. Their fiction has appeared in publications such as The Dread Machine, Cosmic Horror Monthly, Etherea, and The Vanishing Point. They are currently at work on their debut novel. You can find more details about their work at www.keilyblair.com. They live in Tennessee with their husband, dog, cat, and guinea pigs.

E.S. CORBLE

E.S.Corble is a young writer from New Zealand. She's always harbored a deep love of darker fairy tales and myths, and when not writing can be found in the woods seeking creatures we have only ever read about. If your scrying bowl fails you, you can find her at www.tumblr.com/blog/escorble-writes

JONATHAN LOUIS DUCKWORTH

Jonathan Louis Duckworth is a completely normal, entirely human person with the right number of heads and everything. He received his MFA from Florida International University. His speculative fiction work appears in Pseudopod, Beneath Ceaseless Skies, Southwest Review, Flash Fiction Online, and elsewhere. He is a PhD student at University of North Texas where he serves as the interviews editor at American Literary Review, and he is also an active HWA member.

STEPHANIE ELLIS

Stephanie Ellis writes dark speculative prose and poetry and has been published in a variety of magazines and anthologies. Her longer work includes the novels, The Five Turns of the Wheel and Reborn, and the novellas, Bottled and Paused. Her novel, The Woodcutter, is due for release via Brigids Gate Press in 2023. Her dark poetry has been published in her collections Foundlings (co-authored with Cindy O'Quinn), Lilith Rising (co-authored with Shane Douglas Keene) and Metallurgy, as well as the HWA Poetry Showcase Volumes VI, VII, VIII and IX, and Black Spot Books Under Her Skin. She can be found supporting indie authors at HorrorTree.com via the weekly Indie Bookshelf Releases. She is an active member of the HWA and can be found at https://stephanieellis.org, on Twitter at @el_stevie, Instagram stephanieellis7963 and also somewhere on Facebook.

www.stephanieellis.org

S.O. GREEN

S.O. Green (they/them) is a genre-fluid writer living in the Kingdom of Fife with husband, John. They are the chief contract editor and contest judge for Eerie River Publishing, and author of the post-apocalyptic novelette, Sin Chaser, also published by Eerie. They have over 80 short works published with imprints including Dragon Soul Press, Black Ink Fiction and Nordic Press. They are a writer, vegan, martial artist, gamer, and occasionally a terrible person (but only to fictional people).

Website: https://thebasementoflove.blogspot.com/
Facebook: https://www.facebook.com/thebasementoflove
Twitter: https://twitter.com/SOGreenWriter

BITTER KARELLA

Bitter Karella is a genderfluid goblin best known as the creator of the Hugo-nominated microfiction comedy account @ Midnight_Pals which asks what if all your favourite horror writers were to gather around the campfire and tell scary stories like in the classic Nickelodeon series "Are You Afraid of the Dark?" Karella also writes gonzo psycho-sexual body horror with a grotesquely humorous edge. Her short story "Low Tide Jenny," originally published in Seize the Press magazine, was a winner of the Brave New Weird award for best new weird fiction of 2022 by Tenebrous Press. His work has also appeared in Bag of Bones' "Step into the Light," Tenebrous Press' "Your Body is Not Your Body," Ghoulish Books' "Bound in Flesh," and From Beyond Press' "The World Belongs to Us." He's the author and artist of three graphic novels, including a comic adaptation of the Malleus Maleficarum, and co-host of the podcast "A Special Presentation, or Alf Will Not be Seen Tonight" about comic strips adapted into TV specials.

www.bitterkarella.com
Twitter: @bitterkarella

RYAN MARIE KETTERER

Ryan Marie Ketterer is from Malden, Massachusetts. Her work can be found in Dark Matter Magazine and CHM, as well as several anthologies. She's a fan of the weird and uncanny, and her writing draws most of its influence from the works of Shirley Jackson and Thomas Ligotti. When she isn't writing stories, Ryan is writing code for a software startup in Boston, MA or training for another road race. You can find her on Twitter and Instagram at @RyanMarie47.

TJ PRICE

TJ Price's corporeal being is currently located in Raleigh, NC, with his handsome partner of many years, but his ghosts live in north-eastern Connecticut, southern Maine, and North Brooklyn. His work has been published in Coffin Bell Journal, The Bear Creek Gazette and in Pidgeonholes; he also has a novelette (The Disappearance of Tom Nero) forthcoming from Spooky House Press in May 2023. He can be found at tjpricewrites.com or invoked on the blue bird @eerieyore.

BRADLEY DON RICHTER

Bradley Richter grew up on a junk food diet of Stephen King and Dean Koontz before developing a taste for more literary morsels as a literature major at UC Santa Cruz. He lives with his spouse in the Santa Cruz Mountains, where he teaches music, plays mandolin in a bluegrass band, and reads and writes as often as he can. You can read more of his writing and listen to his music by visiting his website and connect with him on Twitter @bradleydrichter.

www.bradleydonrichter.com

JULIE SEVENS

Julie Sevens is a horror writer and an everything reader. The tentacular appendages of the universe have moved her from Ohio to Philadelphia, to Berlin. Now just beyond the interstellar blastzone of Chicago, Julie lives with her husband, two sons, a doorstep spider named Lentil, and a ghost in the closet who resists naming. Find more of her nightmares at juliesevens.com.

TEAGAN OLIVIA STURMER

Teagan Olivia Sturmer is passionate about writing stories of girls and women who are stronger than they know. Short stories of Teagan's can be found in anthologies from Phantom House Press, Quill and Crow Publishing, Shortwave Media, and Eerie River Publishing. Having been diagnosed with General Anxiety Disorder and PTSD for most of her life, Teagan is passionate about telling stories of resilience. Stories of characters who discover the power of their own emotions, and use that power to overcome. Teagan lives in Michigan's wild Upper Peninsula with her husband, Brice, their pups, Rosie and Remus, and one rather persnickety calico cat, Phoebe. She is represented by Amy Giuffrida of the Belcastro Agency.

www.teaganoliviasturmer.com

APRIL YATES

April Yates is the author of the sapphic, historical Gothic romance ASHTHORNE and other strange dark fictions. You can keep up to date with publications at aprilyates.com or find her spouting nonsense and posting inappropriate GIFs on Twitter @April_Yates_

WYNNE F. WINTERS

Wynne F. Winters has been known to dabble in the fantastic and the macabre, sometimes at the same time. They've been published in several horror anthologies, including With Blood and Ash and Of Fire and Stars from Eerie River Publishing. They've also been known to post stories online under the Reddit username u/firesidechats451. If you're interested in hearing their controversial tea opinions, being regaled with grisly true crime details, or finding out when a new story is up, you can follow them on Twitter @WintersWynne.

twitter.com/WintersWynne

Join our newsletter today and download a free book!
https://mailchi.mp/71e45b6d5880/welcomebook

More from Eerie River

Eerie River Publishing, is a small independant publishing house
that is devoted to releasing quality dark fiction books
and anthologies.

To stay up to date with all our new releases and upcoming
giveaways, follow us on Facebook, Twitter, Instagram and
YouTube. Sign up for our monthly newsletter and receive a free
ebook Darkness Reclaimed, as our thank you gift.

https://mailchi.mp/71e45b6d5880/welcomebook

Interested in becoming a Patreon member?
Patreon membership gives you exclusive sneak peeks at
upcoming books, early chapter releases, covers art as well as free
ebooks and discounts on paperbacks.

https://www.patreon.com/EerieRiverPub.

RACHAEL BOUCKER
SHADES
OF
NIGHT
BOOK ONE OF THE NIGHT ORDER SERIES

OF FIRE AND STARS
A DARK FANTASY LGBTQIA+ ANTHOLOGY
AVAILABLE EVERYWHERE